El Diablo

Following a Comanchero raid led by El Carcinero – the Butcher – young Emily Mercer has lost just about everything: her folks, her home and her future. But she'd be damned if she was going to lose her beloved stallion, El Diablo, as well.

With the stallion already sold to Stillman J. Stadtlander – the ruling rancher of Santa Rosa – Emily faces a ruthless opponent, who has the enigmatic gunfighter Latigo Rawlins on his payroll. But she has an ace of her own: a man, known only as Drifter, is backing her every step of the way. And if Emily doesn't get El Diablo back there'll be hell to pay.

El Diablo

Steve Hayes

A Black Horse Western

ROBERT HALE · LONDON

© Steve Hayes 2012
First published in Great Britain 2012

ISBN 978-0-7090-9841-6

Robert Hale Limited
Clerkenwell House
Clerkenwell Green
London EC1R 0HT

www.halebooks.com

Typeset by
Derek Doyle & Associates, Shaw Heath
Printed and bound in Great Britain by
CPI Antony Rowe, Chippenham and Eastbourne

For Richard 'Dick' Shepherd
My agent and long-time friend

CHAPTER ONE

They were less than a mile from the US–Mexican border when they heard the shooting. The tall, wide-shouldered, hard-bellied man known as Drifter reined up and motioned for the young girl riding beside him to do the same.

The rifle fire was coming from a rock-strewn arroyo about one hundred yards ahead. Drifter grabbed his field-glasses from his saddle-bag and trained them on the nearest rocks. He screwed the eyepieces around until suddenly the rocks showed clearly and the man crouched behind them looked close enough to touch.

'Judas,' Drifter said softly.

'What, what?' the girl asked.

'It's Latigo – Latigo Rawlins!'

'The gunfighter you and Mesquite used to ride with?'

'Yeah.' He focused on the men shooting at Latigo from across the arroyo. 'Some Mexicans have got him pinned down.'

'*Bandidos?*'

'Looks like.'

'Then we have to go help him.'

'You,' Drifter said, as she reached for the rifle tucked in the saddle boot, 'are going nowhere.' He pulled out his own rifle, a 45-70 caliber Winchester '86, and pointed to a nearby rocky outcrop. 'Take the mule behind there and stay put till I get back.'

Emily Mercer, a tall, slim, wholesomely pretty fifteen-year-old whose stubbornness often frustrated Drifter, eyed him defiantly. 'Just because you've suddenly decided to admit you're my father,' she said, her voice low and educated, 'doesn't give you the right to order me around.'

There wasn't time to argue. Not if he wanted to help Latigo. So, through gritted teeth, he said, 'Please-wait-for-me-behind-those-rocks.'

'That's better,' she said. Taking the lead-rope from him, she spurred her horse toward the rocky outcrop, the pack-mule grudgingly following.

CHAPTER TWO

Hunched over the sorrel's neck, Drifter galloped across the scrubland to the arroyo. There he reined up beside a clump of mesquite growing along the nearest bank and slid from the saddle. Ducked low, he ran for the rocks protecting Latigo Rawlins.

The Mexicans, who were dressed more like ranchers than *bandidos*, opened fire at him. Bullets kicked up the sand around his feet. Trying to make himself less of a target, Drifter zigzagged as he ran. But running wasn't his forte. He was too tall and rangy and his long legs were slightly bowed from a life in the saddle. A good shot would have nailed him. But fortunately for him, the Mexicans were poor marksmen. He made it safely to the rocks and dived to the ground beside the handsome little bounty hunter.

Latigo fired his Sharps-Borchardt rifle, Model 1878 at his attackers, who were peppering him from the brush across the arroyo, then rolled over and sat with his back against the rocks while he reloaded. 'I don't know where the hell you came from,' he said, grinning at Drifter, 'but I'm mighty glad to see you.'

'Figured you would be—' Drifter broke off, ducking as a bullet ricocheted off a rock near his head. 'Nice company you keep.'

'*Bandidos de montana*,' Latigo said, referring to the bandits that inhabited the sierras.

Drifter frowned, surprised. 'They're a long way from home.'

'Yeah. Pickin's must be slim. Bastards have been doggin' my trail ever since I left Palomas.'

Drifter aimed at the tip of a high-crowned sombrero poking above the brush, lowered his sights a little and fired. There was a sharp cry of pain and the brush quivered as the wounded man crawled away. 'How many you figure?'

'Six, maybe eight. They jumped me 'bout a half mile south of here. There was twelve of 'em then. I made it this far 'fore they shot my horse out from under me.' He thumbed at the carcass of a dead roan sprawled nearby. 'Been here ever since. You alone?' he added.

'Uh-uh. Got a girl with me.' He nodded toward the rocky outcrop. 'She's back there holding the horses.'

'Since when'd you start ridin' with women?'

'Since when'd you start asking questions?'

Latigo chuckled. Facing front, he fired at a figure crouched behind a clump of ocotillo growing on the opposite bank. The figure yelped, rose to its knees then fell on its face. Dead.

Immediately the other Mexicans all fired in unison. Their bullets spattered the rocks near Drifter and Latigo, forcing them to keep their heads down.

'How long you figuring on putting up with this?' Drifter asked.

Latigo shrugged. At five feet five, he was wiry, cat-quick and boyishly handsome. Freckles and curly sandy hair added to his youthful appearance, and as usual he was wearing an expensive city-bought shirt and hand-tooled, high-heeled cowboy boots. Two ivory-grip Colt .44s poked from black-leather holsters that were tied down, gunfighter-fashion. But it was his eyes that caught everyone's attention: they were a wolfish yellow and full of menace.

'I'm open to any suggestion,' he said.

'Cover me,' Drifter said, handing him his Winchester. Waiting for Latigo to open fire, he jumped up and ran to his sorrel, pulled something from a saddle-bag and came sprinting back.

'Jesus,' Latigo said, as he saw what Drifter was holding. 'First women and now dynamite? You've gotten mighty salty since we last rode together.'

'And you've gotten mighty talkative,' Drifter grumbled. He hurled the dynamite across the arroyo so that the stick landed in front of a large clump of juniper and brush behind which most of the Mexicans were firing. In the same motion he drew, aimed and fired his Colt .45.

The bullet struck the dynamite, exploding it.

Cries of pain mingled with the roar of the explosion. And as the dirt and stones rained back to earth several injured Mexicans lurched to their feet and started to stagger away.

Latigo drew one of his .44 Colts and gunned them

11

down before they had taken more than a few steps.

Two more men rose from nearby bushes, dropped their guns and raised their hands in surrender.

Latigo gunned them down, too.

It was over almost before the noise of the explosion had faded.

'I owe you one,' the dandy little Texan told Drifter.

'You would've done the same for me.'

'Let's hope it never comes to that,' Latigo said. He grinned boyishly and covered his curly sandy hair with a custom-made, pearl-gray Stetson. 'Now whyn't you go round-up your woman while I make sure all of them bastards are lyin' feet-up.' Rising, he started down the bank of the arroyo, reloading his Colt as he went.

CHAPTER THREE

When Latigo returned from the other side of the arroyo, he was surprised to find Drifter talking to a young girl who was letting her horse drink out of her cupped hands.

Latigo had never seen her before and wondered what the hell Drifter was doing in Mexico with a young girl; especially one who wasn't Mexican. Knowing Drifter as he did, he knew she was too young to be his girlfriend. So who was she? He studied her carefully as he approached and what he saw piqued his interest. Though her farm-fresh sunburned face was smudged with dirt, her long brown hair tangled, and her boy's shirt and jeans trail-soiled, she somehow still managed to appear feminine and ladylike. This was no tomboy! And when she spoke it was in a cultured manner that seemed out of place in these desolate surroundings.

'What I do not understand,' she said, sounding more like forty than fifteen, 'is where you acquired the dynamite from. I thought you'd used the last of it when the Comancheros attacked us.'

'I thought so too,' Drifter said. 'But last time we gave the horses a blow, I happened to look in my saddle-bags and saw one stick remaining.' He shrugged, still puzzled. 'I must have missed it somehow.' He paused as he saw Latigo approaching with his usual swagger; then waiting till the mercurial, diminutive gunfighter came up, he introduced them.

'Emily, this is Mr Rawlins. Latigo, my daughter, Emily.'

'Daughter?' Latigo frowned, surprised. 'Who you tryin' to kid?'

'No one. Emily really is my daughter.'

'Yeah?' Latigo scratched his head. 'Hell, I didn't know you had any young'uns, Quint.'

'Yeah ... well. ...' Drifter said, stumped for an answer.

Emily came to his rescue. 'That's because I am away at school most of the time,' she said. Wiping one wet hand on her jeans, she offered it to Latigo. 'Nice to meet you, Mr Rawlins.'

Latigo shook hands and politely tipped his hat. 'Miss Emily.' Then, turning to Drifter, said, 'Truth is, *amigo*, I never even knew you were hitched.'

Drifter shrugged non-committally, 'What can I say?' and brushed his long black hair out of his lean, hawkish face. It was a habit of his, something he did when he felt uneasy; and now, anxious to end the conversation, he started to walk away.

Latigo stopped him. 'Your wife – she from around Santa Rosa?'

Drifter shook his head, his fierce gray eyes narrowing

14

uneasily. An awkward pause followed.

'I'd like to meet her sometime,' Latigo said. 'Any gal who could wrassle you to the altar must be like holdin' four aces!'

Again Drifter was stumped for words.

Emily said quietly, 'My mother is dead.'

Latigo lowered his odd-colored amber eyes and awkwardly twisted his hat in his hand. 'Sorry to hear that, missy.'

'Thank you. It has been difficult, but I am slowly getting over it. Now, if you'll please excuse me. . . .' Turning, she carried her canteen to the pack mule standing nearby and began to give it water.

'She's mighty polite,' Latigo said, watching Emily go. 'Refined lookin', too. You're a lucky fella, Quint.'

'I know. Emily is something special. By the way,' Drifter added. 'I don't know where you're headed, but you're welcome to take the mule.'

'Thanks. Mules ain't my style. But I'd be obliged if I could borrow your horse an' go round up one of them Mexican broncs. They're short on the looks, but long on stamina.'

'Good idea. But I'll go while you stay with Emily,' Drifter said, stepping into the saddle. 'Wilson doesn't react kindly to strangers and—' He broke off as the irascible golden sorrel, with its contrasting flaxen mane and tail, swung its head around and nipped at his leg. Drifter jerked his Apache knee-high moccasin from the stirrup, just avoiding the snapping teeth, and slapped the horse with his sweat-stained campaign hat. 'Damn your miserable hide,' he cursed.

15

'Horse of mine ever did that,' Latigo said, 'I'd put a round 'tween its eyes 'fore it took another breath.'

'Don't think it ain't crossed my mind,' Drifter said. Then to Emily, 'Be right back.' He kicked up the leggy sorrel and man and horse descended the steep bank and started across the arroyo.

CHAPTER FOUR

While they waited for Drifter to return, the two of them sat talking in the shade beside the same rocky outcrop Emily had hidden behind earlier.

Latigo, who normally kept to himself, was intrigued enough by Emily to ask where she went to school. St. Marks, she replied, in Las Cruces. She went on to explain that it was a boarding school run by nuns, then added that she wasn't actually going to school right now. The Mother Superior had let her take time off to bury her family and recover her horses. Once she sold her ranch outside Santa Rosa, however, she intended to go back and finish her classes. 'How about you, Mr Rawlins?' she enquired. 'What are you doing down here in Chihuahua?'

'Trackin' a fugitive from Yuma prison.'

'Oh, that's right. You're a bounty hunter, aren't you?'

' 'Mong other things.'

'Think you'll ever catch up with him?'

'Already did.' Latigo rolled a smoke, put it between his sun-cracked lips and flared a match. 'Right now he's buzzard bait.'

' 'Mean you shot him?'

'Right 'fore he tried to shoot me.'

Emily didn't say anything. But seeing her look of distaste, Latigo felt an uncharacteristic need to explain.

'Wasn't murder, missy, if that's what you're thinkin'.'

Emily shrugged. 'It is not my business to judge, Mr Rawlins.'

He found her reply strange for one so young.

'I caught up with the SOB in a cantina in Palomas. He saw me first and threw down on me.'

'But you were too quick for him?'

Latigo lazily blew a smoke ring and poked his finger through it before saying laconically: ' 'Bout covers it.'

'I guess Drifter – I mean, Quint – my father was right. You really are fast with a gun.'

'More than fast,' Latigo corrected. 'The fastest ever was.'

'Truly?'

'Truly.'

'Boy,' Emily said, impressed. 'You must spend your whole life practising, Mr Rawlins.'

Latigo shook his head. 'Don't need to. It's a gift...' He looked at his left hand. 'Some folks are born to paint or write books – me, I was born with a gun in my hand. Watch. . . .'

Emily watched.

Latigo tensed.

Emily *thought* she saw him move but wasn't sure. But she was sure about the next thing she saw – a gun that appeared almost magically in his left hand.

'Oh my goodness,' she breathed. 'H-How did you do that?'

'I dunno,' he said simply. 'I just do it.' He holstered his six-gun, again his movement so fast it almost defied reason, and added: 'What else did Quint tell you 'bout me?'

'Not much. Just that you, he, Mesquite Jennings and another man – I can't remember his name – all rode together once.'

'That'd be Ben Lawless.'

'That's right.'

'Anythin' else?'

'No. But when they stopped talking about you, Mesquite mentioned Mr Lawless again.'

'Go on.'

'He told my father that after his girlfriend, Cally, was raped and killed by Slade Stadtlander and the Iverson brothers, he and Mr Lawless ended up courting the same widow—'

'Ingrid Bjorkman.'

'Y-Yes, I think that was her name. Said compared with the other women in and around Santa Rosa, she was—'

'Like a rose among thorns?'

'Yes! That's exactly what he said.'

'He ain't exaggeratin'. She's one fine-lookin' woman. Got a daughter 'bout your age, too.'

'Yes. Mesquite told me. Raven. Said once, when he was shot, she was the one who went and fetched this Mescalero healer who saved his life.'

Latigo nodded, 'Name's Lolotea. Means Gift from

19

God in Apache,' and he ran his fingers through his curly yellow hair.

Emily said, 'I'm glad she saved him. I know he's an outlaw, but I really like Mesquite. In fact I wish he would have come back with us to Santa Rosa.'

'He can't. They'd hang him.'

'Yes, for a Morgan stallion he didn't steal. But I guess you already know that.'

Latigo shrugged. 'What I know is that Gabe – that's his real name, in case you didn't know: Gabriel Moonlight – swears he won Brandy fair an' square in a poker game.'

'It's true. Drift— my father told me so and he would not lie. Said that Mr Stadtlander hates to lose so much, he decided to get Brandy back by claiming Mesquite stole him—'

'Worse'n that. He got that two-cent puppet sheriff of his, Lonnie Forbes, to go after Gabe with a rope.'

The mention of Sheriff Forbes made Emily feel sad. 'You should not speak ill of the dead, you know.'

'Forbes is *dead?*'

'Yes. Two days ago. Comancheros killed him.'

'Whoa, whoa.' Latigo raised his hand. 'Slow down, little lady. Forbes was sheriff of Santa Rosa. He had no authority down here in Chihuahua.'

'He wasn't sheriff anymore. He turned in his star so he could help me get my horses back. . . .' She went on to explain that Comancheros had murdered her family, stolen their prize stallion, El Diablo, and all their breed mares, and driven them across the border to sell in Mexico. They probably would have killed her, too she added, if she had not been away at school.

Latigo looked puzzled. 'If Quint's your pa, who's this "family" you're talkin' about?'

'The Mercers.'

'Frank Mercer, the horse-rancher?'

'Yes.'

'I've heard Quint talk highly about him. An' your ma. Never told me he had a child by her, though.'

'Never told me either. No one did. Was not until after they were all killed that Quint said *he* was my father. It was quite a shock, as you can imagine. I mean, despite the fact that he often stopped at our ranch to water his horse, and he and my folks were friends, I knew very little about him – except once I did ask him why he always wore soldier's pants instead of jeans and he said that when he was younger he had been a scout with the Fourth Cavalry. . . .' She paused, as if to collect her thoughts, then with a slightly trembling lower lip said, 'It was the army who found my family – their bodies I mean. They told Sheriff Forbes who wired me the news and the next day I came home for the funeral. That's when I heard about the stolen horses and tried to hire some gunmen to help me find the Comancheros and recover them. But before I could find any takers, the sheriff offered to go with me instead.' She paused, decided to leave out the part about signing the deed to her ranch over to Forbes as payment, and said, 'We made it all the way to Palomas. Then these two outlaws jumped us. That's when Quint and Mesquite rode up and shot them.'

Latigo frowned, confused. ''Mean they just happened

21

to show up?'

'Yes. Well, not really. According to my father, he had been following me from Santa Rosa – you know, to keep an eye on me. Mesquite happened to be with him and since he knew where the Comanchero stronghold was, he agreed to help us.' She paused as she saw his expression before saying, 'I know it all sounds very confusing, but it's the gospel truth. One thing just happened after another and—'

'What about your horses?'

Emily hesitated, wondering how to explain without making her story even more complicated. 'Well, I never did get my stallion back. *El Carnicero* – the leader of the Comancheros – had already sold him. But we did round up all the mares. Trouble was we had to come back through Blanco Canyon, where these *bandidos* were waiting to kill us, so I ended up giving them the mares in exchange for our lives.'

'You were lucky,' Latigo said, flipping his cigarette away. 'Not many folks ever make it through Blanco Canyon and live to tell about it.' He stopped as they heard a rider approaching. Motioning for Emily to keep still, he peered around the rocks. Riding toward him was Drifter, leading one of the *bandidos'* horses.

'It's all right,' Latigo said. 'It's just your pa.'

Emily looked relieved. 'Good. We will be riding on soon.'

CHAPTER FIVE

It was late afternoon when the three of them rode across the border at Columbus, New Mexico. A tiny sun-baked village named after the great explorer, it would become famous in 1916 as the place where Pancho Villa and his forces raided US soil in retaliation for lack of promised support from President Woodrow Wilson.

But presently, as Drifter, Emily and Latigo rode along a narrow dirt trail that served as a street, Columbus was famous for nothing but swirling dust storms and scorching heat. Located just north of the Arizona & Southwestern Railroad tracks it consisted of a few stores, some scattered adobe shacks and a rundown cantina.

'You hungry?' Drifter asked Emily as they approached the cantina.

'Not enough to eat here,' she replied.

'Then we'll keep riding and chow down when we camp tonight. That OK with you?' Drifter added to Latigo.

'Sure.'

23

'How far you riding with us, anyway?'

'Till we reach the east trail out of Santa Rosa.'

Drifter frowned, puzzled. 'That trail only leads to one place: Stillman Stadtlander's spread.'

'I know,' Latigo said casually. 'I got business with the man.'

Drifter bristled. 'This "business" – it wouldn't have anything to do with the thousand dollars he's offering for Gabe's head, would it?'

'You know me better'n that, *amigo*.'

'Do I?'

Latigo smiled affably – a misleading smile that never reached his menacing yellow eyes. 'It's a mite warm to be on the prod,' he said softly.

'Then tell me why the hell you were in Mexico.'

Sensing a potentially dangerous showdown, Emily said quickly, 'Mr Rawlins was after a convict who escaped from Yuma prison.'

'That for true?' Drifter pressed.

Latigo tapped his shirt pocket. 'Maybe you'd like to see the warrant out on him signed by the warden.'

'No,' Drifter said, calming. 'I'll take your word for it. I would like to know why you're being so goddamn affable, though. It ain't like you, Lefty.'

'It's this God-awful heat,' Latigo said, slipping Emily a wink. 'It's fried my brains an' sapped all the meanness out of me.'

They rode on in silence, the sun sinking behind the Sierras but still hot enough to warm the south-west side of their bodies. Soon Columbus fell behind them, its silhouette lost in the oncoming lemony-violet dusk.

Ahead, lay a vast open scrubland that eventually would take them to Santa Rosa.

They rode until dark and then made camp inside the ruins of an abandoned adobe *rancho*. Over the years relentless desert winds had blown off most of the roof and sandstorms had worn the walls down to smooth, misshapen lumps. Neither offered much shelter against a sudden summer rainstorm that struck moments after Drifter and Latigo unsaddled the horses and Emily got a fire going.

Pulling on their slickers, the three of them huddled together in one corner of the old, once-grand *casa*, under what was left of the roof and waited for the downpour to stop.

Ten minutes later the lashing rain ceased as suddenly as it had started. Muddy rivulets streamed along the ruts in the parched red earth and puddles lay everywhere. The cool damp night air became permeated with fragrant desert scents.

A crisp mountain-born breeze sprang up. It chased the dark clouds away, revealing a silvery half-moon that was bright enough to see by.

The three got to their feet and shook the moisture off their slickers.

'Mmm-mmm,' said Emily, sniffing. 'Don't you just love the desert after a rain?'

'I'd sooner have a hot meal,' Drifter grumbled. He kicked the now-soaked firewood, adding to Emily, 'I'll go see if I can find anything dry enough to burn while you open the beans, OK?'

She nodded and, on impulse, called after him,

'Don't let the bats get you.'

Drifter didn't respond. But Latigo, standing nearby, chuckled softly.

Hearing him, Emily blushed. 'Momma always used to say that if I or my brothers went outside after dark. I don't know why, because we seldom ever saw a bat around our place, but—' She broke off, voice choked with emotion, and hurried outside the walls so that Latigo wouldn't see her crying.

The little shootist moved to what was left of the arched doorway, which was still dripping, and spoke to her back. 'It's all right,' he said gently. 'Ain't no shame in grievin' over lost loved ones.'

Emily nodded to show she'd heard him and stood there, fighting back her tears. She was silent a long time. Then her shoulders stopped heaving and she said in a small, innocent voice, 'W-when I first read Sheriff Forbes's wire saying they were all dead, I thought I would *never* stop crying. I cried all that day in class and all that night in the dorm and all during mass the next morning. Then when Sister Celeste took me to the station, I suddenly stopped, you know, as if I'd run out of tears; and from then on, while I was on the train and afterwards, even during the funeral, I did not cry again. Didn't even want to. Not until just now. Isn't that strange?' she added, turning to face him.

'Everything 'bout death is strange,' Latigo said grimly. 'Death has no rules, plays no favorites, and knows no mercy.' He paused, then as if surprised by the thought that had struck him, said, 'Kinda like me.'

'I don't believe that,' Emily said, facing him. 'I

believe, deep down, you are a compassionate, decent man, Mr Rawlins.'

Latigo chuckled mirthlessly. 'You're on a mighty short list.' He turned and disappeared behind the walls.

Emily wiped her tear-stained cheeks with her sleeve and seeing a large puddle a few steps away, went to it and knelt, cupped her hands and scooped up some water. Splashing it over her face, she went to dip her hands into the water again – when a shot was fired behind her.

Startled, she gasped and then recoiled as the bullet struck something in the puddle only inches from her hands.

'Don't move,' Latigo warned. He appeared beside her, Colt in hand.

Emily obeyed, watching with disbelief and horror as a stubby, stout-bodied lizard thrashed momentarily in the water and then lay still.

Latigo used the toe of his boot to flip the dead lizard out of the puddle. It was orange with splotchy black markings and Emily recognized it immediately. Jumping up, she pressed herself against Latigo, the realization of how close to a possible fatal bite she'd been making her tremble.

'Easy,' Latigo said gently. 'It's dead. Can't hurt you—' He stopped as Drifter came charging up.

'What the hell—?' Drifter began.

'Gila monster,' Latigo said, indicating the dead lizard. Then as Emily disengaged herself and turned to Drifter, 'They like to immerse themselves in puddles after a summer rain.'

'I-I'm sorry,' Emily said to Drifter. 'I didn't see it and. . . .'

'It's OK. No harm done.' Drifter stepped close and put an arm about her shoulders. 'Just be more careful in future.'

She nodded and pulling away, said, 'Did you find any dry wood?'

'Yeah, it's over there' – he pointed – 'where I dropped it.' He waited until she had hurried off and then said to Latigo, 'Now I owe you one, *amigo.*'

'Turnabout's fair play,' Latigo said. He grinned and picking up the dead Gila monster, added, 'Reckon now we got meat to go with them beans.'

CHAPTER SIX

The next morning they rose before sunup. It was cold enough to make them shiver but already a warm wind out of Mexico was whipping loose sand against the adobe walls.

Breakfasting on the last of the coffee, beans and biscuits, they saddled up and started out across the arid wasteland. The sky was almost colorless, a sort of pale watery oatmeal with the undersides of the easterly clouds tinted pink and yellow by the approaching dawn. There'd been another brief rainstorm during the night and the damp morning air smelled fresh and clean. But Drifter, anticipating another broiling day and wanting to cover as much ground as possible before the sun hammered them, insisted the horses keep to a brisk, mile-consuming lope.

By late morning they were within ten miles of Santa Rosa. Stopping to give the horses a final blow, they drank from their canteens, the water warm and metallic-tasting, and were about to climb back into the saddle when they heard distant shooting. It came from behind a low scrub-covered rise about a quarter of a mile east of them – an exchange of rifle fire followed by silence, then a few scattered shots that suggested the fight was between a small number of shooters.

Latigo stood up in his stirrups, listening, and then looked at Drifter. 'What do you figure – a huntin' party?'

'Since when did animals start shooting back?'

'What then – someone cornered by a posse?'

'Or a dry-gulching.'

'Two in twenty-four hours – hell's fire, what're the odds of that?'

'In other words, you want us to pretend it isn't happening and keep riding?'

'Why not? Could be some young bucks jumped the reservation. They see your daughter, here, an'—'

'Never mind about me,' Emily broke in. 'I can handle myself.'

'Be sure'n mention that when they drag you off by a rope,' Latigo said.

Drifter hesitated, concerned, and then turned to say something to Emily.

'Don't you dare tell me to wait here,' she warned.

'Wouldn't dream of it,' Drifter said over Latigo's chuckle. 'But you'd be doing me a big favor if you'd lag behind a little. You know. Until we at least know what's going on.'

'Very well,' she said. 'Since you put it nicely, I can do that.'

Drifter rolled his eyes at Latigo, who grinned; then all three mounted up and rode toward the distant rise.

*

A few minutes later Drifter, Latigo and Emily, who was leading the pack-mule, crested the rise and looked down the other side. Below, a long rock-strewn slope flattened out after a half-mile or so into a broad valley, through which snaked an old stagecoach trail that since the arrival of the railroad was seldom used.

Drifter trained his field-glasses on a horseless wagon that was overturned beside the trail. Supplies had been dumped out and spilled flour whitened the ground around a ripped sack. Nearby stood the two-horse team, their panicked flight stopped when the trailing reins had snagged on some rocks.

Two women were crouched behind the wagon. Drifter focused on one and found he was looking at an attractive, fair-skinned woman in her early thirties with sun-streaked tawny hair pulled back in a bun who was reloading an old single-action Colt. Not recognizing her, he shifted focus to the second woman – only to discover that she was a girl, a year or so younger than Emily. Boyishly slim and burned brown as tobacco by the sun, she was grubby-looking with gleaming crow-black hair cut mannishly short and a high-cheek-boned face that despite the peril she and her mother were facing, showed no fear. Armed with a Henry .44 caliber, lever-action, breech-loading rifle, she was taking her time to find a target before shooting – and the fact that her attackers were not rushing them was a tribute to her accuracy.

Across the trail from the wagon, five disheveled,

31

bearded gunmen were hunkered down among the rocks, all of them firing at will at the women. Drifter panned over them and realized they were nothing more than border trash.

'Recognize anyone?' Latigo asked.

'Uh-uh.' Drifter handed him the glasses. 'You?'

Latigo needed only a quick look at the women behind the wagon to say: 'You ain't gonna believe this. It's Gabe's woman!'

'Who?'

'The widow Bjorkman – and her daughter, Raven.'

'We'd better get down there.'

'First let's even the odds some. . . .' Latigo dismounted, took a specially-made telescopic sight from his saddle-bag and attached it his rifle. Then kneeling, he adjusted the lens, took careful aim and squeezed the trigger. The Sharps-Borchardt bucked against his shoulder and Drifter, glasses to his eyes, saw one of the gunmen crumple and lay still. His cohorts were too busy firing at the women to notice him die; and a second man, crouched behind a nearby rock, died before a third gunman noticed they were being shot at from behind. Whirling around, he gazed up at the hilltop and saw Drifter, Latigo and Emily lined along the crest. He yelled to his friends, alerting them – only to then fall backward, rifle dropping, as Latigo's bullet punched a hole in his forehead.

Panicking, the two remaining gunmen blazed away at Latigo. In their hurry they missed him. Jumping up, they ran to their horses tethered nearby.

Calmly, Latigo reloaded and shot one in the back just

as he was mounting. The other gunman managed to at least get mounted before Latigo's next shot knocked him out of the saddle.

Latigo smiled, smugly pleased with himself, and told Drifter: 'Next time you run into Gabe, tell him he owes me a box of shells.'

'If you're right about his woman,' Drifter said wryly, 'he'll probably throw in a bottle of tequila.'

Emily wasn't amused. 'Did you have to kill them all?' she asked Latigo. 'I mean, those last two were trying to escape.'

'Miss Emily,' the little Texan said softly. ''Fore you get much older you better learn one thing: scum like that, they don't deserve to live.'

'Maybe,' she said. 'But isn't it up to God to decide?'

Latigo gave a tight-lipped smile that would have frightened a rattlesnake.

'That's another thing you gotta learn, missy. Never count on God. 'Cause even if He does exist, which ain't likely, most times He's asleep at the reins.' Turning away, he slid his rifle into the saddle boot, stepped into the saddle and guided his horse down the slope toward the overturned wagon.

Emily swung up on to her horse and looked across at Drifter, who was already mounted. 'You think he's right, Quint?'

Drifter shrugged. 'When it comes to blind faith,' he said, 'I'm still on the fence.' Reaching out he took the lead rope from her and nudged the sorrel forward, down the slope, the sleepy-looking pack mule following without complaint.

Emily stared after her father, her religious upbringing arguing with common sense. Then realizing it was a never-ending battle, she gripped the reins tightly and heeled her horse forward, on down the slope.

CHAPTER SEVEN

Raven and her mother, having watched the five gunmen killed, now came from behind the overturned wagon to greet their saviors. Both women were bruised and scratched from being thrown out of the runaway wagon, but otherwise unharmed.

Raven recognized Latigo first and exclaimed, 'Momma, it's that gunfighter Gabe knows!'

'So I see,' Ingrid Bjorkman said. She'd met Latigo several times, and had never liked him. Or trusted him. And though she was deeply grateful to him for saving them, she wished it had been someone else. 'What about the other man and the girl – do you know who they are?'

'Never seen 'em before. C'mon. . . .' Raven started forward.

'Stay here,' Ingrid began – then stopped as Raven ignored her and ran to meet Latigo Rawlins. Ingrid sighed, irked by her fiercely independent daughter's disobedience. Then in an effort to look presentable, she brushed a wisp of sun-colored hair from her face and dusted herself off before following Raven.

After introductions, Drifter and Latigo tied their ropes to the two upturned wheels and backed their horses up until the wagon righted itself. Fortunately, neither the tongue nor axles were broken. While Emily and Raven attached the team to the wagon, the two men helped Ingrid put the supplies in back. Most of the flour had spilled on to the ground. But what was left in the sack was unspoiled and after tying a string around the neck, Drifter placed the sack on the seat between Ingrid and Raven and then stepped back to get a better look at the woman whom Gabriel Moonlight risked getting hanged for each time he crossed the border to see her.

Small and slim, she had large blue eyes, fine, almost delicate features and a full-lipped mouth shaped for smiling. Though the squint lines at the corners of her eyes and her tanned skin indicated she was no new-comer to the desert, she exuded an aura of gentility that didn't fit the harsh environment – in much the same way, Drifter thought, as Emily's elegance belied her early ranch-style upbringing.

Raven, on the other hand, looked as if she'd been born to the desert. There was a defiant, untamed look about her. It was especially noticeable in the depths of her big black eyes, eyes that made him think of a wild creature. Or an Apache, he thought. That reminded him of another time when, a few years back, he had sat opposite the famous Chiricahua warrior woman, *Dahteste*, at a council meeting; and thinking as he met the gaze of this beautiful but dangerous Apache, that

36

he was looking into the eyes of an eagle or a wolf.

A voice interrupted his thoughts and he realized Latigo was talking to him. 'He wasn't wounded when you last saw him, right?'

'No,' Emily answered, realizing that Drifter hadn't been listening. 'Mesquite – I mean Gabe was fine. In fact I asked him to come with us, Mrs Bjorkman,' she added, wondering why Raven was glaring at her jealously, 'but he refused. But he did say that one day he would track me down, didn't he, Quint?'

Drifter nodded, 'That he did,' and smiled reassuringly at Ingrid. 'I wouldn't worry about Gabe, ma'am. As you must know by now, he's more than capable of looking after himself.'

'I do indeed,' Ingrid said in a voice as gentle as her nature. 'But I also know that he takes too many risks, unnecessary risks, I might add, because he thinks he can thumb his nose at the law and get away with it.'

'It's your fault,' Raven grumbled. 'If you'd pick up stakes and move to Chihuahua, like he keeps askin' us to, Gabe wouldn't be in any danger.'

'Mind your manners,' Ingrid snapped. 'I've told you before: you're too young to be addressing adults by their first name.'

'But I call him Gabe all the time when you ain't around and he don't mind a bit.'

'I don't care. *I* mind, and that's all that matters. And don't say *ain't*. I've taught you better than that.'

'Goodgodalmighty,' Raven muttered.

'That's enough! Now get on that wagon. We have to go back to town and buy more flour, and I want to be home before dark. Go on,' she said as Raven defied her. 'Do as I tell you!' Waiting for her daughter to grudgingly climb on to the wagon seat, she then said to Latigo and Drifter: 'I don't know how to thank you, either of you. I hate to think what those men would've done to us if you hadn't stopped them.'

'No need to thank me,' Drifter said. 'Latigo, here, did all the shooting.'

Latigo smiled smugly, but didn't say anything.

'Next time you come by our place to water your horse,' Raven blurted, anxious to get attention, 'Momma will bake you the best berry pie you ever ate.'

'I'll consider that full payment, missy,' Latigo said. Then to Ingrid, 'We're headed for Santa Rosa. Maybe you should ride along with us, ma'am.'

'We'd be delighted to,' she said. 'This isn't the first time we've had trouble with drifters.'

Emily looked at Drifter and suppressed a smile. 'They certainly can pose a problem,' she admitted. 'But every once in a while, one comes along that makes up for all the others. Isn't that right – *Father?*'

It was the first time she had ever addressed him that way and, despite the fact that she said it, tongue-in-cheek, Drifter felt a surge of pride.

'If you say so, Daughter,' he said.

CHAPTER EIGHT

The east trail wasn't really a trail at all. It was a broad, dry river-bed that thousands of years ago had been a fast-flowing tributary of the Rio Grande. It snaked its dusty way west, across the flat, scorched scrubland and on through the southern outskirts of Santa Rosa – a small but fast-growing town that in 1848, when the Mexican-American War ended and Mexico ceded the South-west and California to the United States, was just a tiny pueblo inhabited by Mexicans and a few Christianized Manso Indians.

After leaving Santa Rosa the wash joined an old wagon and stagecoach trail, forming a natural fork, then meandered on until it reached the south-eastern corner of Stillman J. Stadtlander's vast cattle ranch. There, it narrowed into a dry creek and eventually became lost in the distant foothills.

Now, as Drifter and the others came to the fork, Latigo reined up and said, 'Here's where I leave you, folks.' He tipped his hat to Ingrid. 'Nice seein' you again, Mrs Bjorkman.'

'You too,' she said. 'And again, thank you so much for helping us.'

'Don't forget about the pie,' Raven chimed in.

'Count on it,' Latigo said. He waited for Ingrid and Raven to ride on in the wagon, then turned to Emily. 'Hope I see you soon, missy.'

'I hope so too,' she replied, smiling. Then, sensing Drifter wanted a few private words with Latigo, she told him to, 'Catch up with us', and rode after the Bjorkmans.

Latigo watched her go with a tinge of regret. 'Reckon you're gonna have your hands full from now on,' he said to Drifter.

'Seems like. But then, I have a lot of years of parenting to make up for.'

'I envy you them,' Latigo said. For a rare moment his handsome boyish face clouded with sadness. Then, brightening, he said, 'Anythin' ever happens to you, Quint, I'll be there for Emily. Count on it.'

'I'll be sure to tell her that,' Drifter said, surprised that the cold-blooded little gunfighter could care for anyone. Then, giving a quick throwaway salute, 'Be seeing you, *amigo*,' he spurred his horse after Emily and the Bjorkmans.

'I'm sure you will,' Latigo said under his breath. And the way he said it didn't bode well for Drifter's future.

It was late afternoon but still oven-hot when Drifter, Emily, Ingrid and Raven entered Santa Rosa. The town was bustling with activity. The stockyards alongside the train tracks were full of sleepy, dung-smelling cattle, all wearing Stillman J. Stadtlander's Double S brand; Front and Main Street were filled with riders and horse-drawn traffic, and the recently installed sidewalks fronting all the stores, offices, restaurants and cantinas swarmed with businessmen, cowboys, miners and townspeople.

Ingrid reined up her team beside an alley separating McConklin's Hardware Store from Melvin's Haberdashery and turned to Drifter, riding alongside her. 'I don't want to impose, but if you and your daughter are thirsty, I would love to buy you both refreshments.'

'Well,' Drifter began.

'Oh, please, it's the least I can do, after what you did for us. Besides, there's a new restaurant just opened up on the next corner – Lilian's. The owner's from back East – New York, I think. It's not exactly like the Harvey House in Deming, but it does serve sarsaparilla and even that new soft drink from Philadelphia, Hires' root beer.'

'Emily?' Drifter said, looking at his daughter. 'What do you say?'

'Sounds wonderful,' she said politely.

'I'm thirsty too,' Raven said, irked that she wasn't asked. ' 'Case anyone's interested.'

'Then lead the way, young lady,' Drifter said. He hid a knowing wink to Ingrid, as if empathizing with how hard it was to raise her rebellious daughter, and then he and Emily escorted the wagon on along Main Street to the restaurant.

Inside, Lilian's was small, elegant and comfortably furnished. The hard-back chairs were padded with

41

green-and-gold brocade, the snowy tablecloths were made of Irish linen and the young, polite waitresses wore black uniforms and starched white aprons not unlike the famous Harvey Girls.

One of them led Drifter, Ingrid and the girls to a table beside the big lace-curtained window facing the Carlisle Hotel across the street. After they had ordered, Drifter told Emily that since it was getting late, rather than ride out to her ranch they would spend the night at the hotel.

'Isn't that a waste of money?' she said frugally. 'I mean we're going to need every cent we have if we're going to rebuild the ranch—' She stopped as Drifter reacted to the man who'd just entered; then turning, she looked at the newcomer herself. Almost as tall as Drifter, he had even broader shoulders, lean hips, and the same air of confidence. His dark hair was neatly trimmed as was the mustache he'd grown to make him seem older than his twenty-four years. He wore a black, flat-brimmed hat and looked lean and hard in a black suit and black string-tie. An ebony-grip Colt .45 poked from the holster on his right hip and pinned on his vest was a deputy US marshal's badge.

'You know him?' Emily asked her father.

Drifter nodded. 'Ezra Macahan – out of El Paso.'

'Did he come here to arrest you?' Raven said to Drifter.

'Raven!' Ingrid looked aghast. 'How dare you! Now apologize at once!'

'Why?' Raven demanded. 'I was just askin'.'

'You don't ask people things like that,' Ingrid

42

scolded. 'It's very rude and offensive—'

'It's all right,' Drifter said, amused. 'I'm not offended. No, Macahan's not after me,' he told Raven. 'And I'm mighty glad he ain't.'

'How come?'

'Dear God,' Ingrid breathed. 'What'd I just tell you about asking questions?'

'How'm I s'posed to learn stuff I don't know if I don't ask questions?' Raven said, scowling.

'You could try books,' Emily suggested. 'Or ask your teacher at school.'

'I don't go to school,' Raven said, happy to be the center of attention. 'Since Pa was killed, Momma teaches me to read an' write an' add numbers at home.'

'But apparently I can't teach you any manners,' Ingrid said darkly. 'Please forgive her,' she added to Drifter. 'She doesn't mean to be rude. It's just that she has an insatiable appetite for learning.'

'Nothing to forgive,' he said. Then to Raven, 'I'm glad the marshal's not after me, because although he's still young he's already got a reputation for always getting his man.' He paused as Macahan, on recognizing his voice, now came up to Drifter.

'I thought that was you, Longley—'

'Good to see you, Macahan.' Drifter rose and shook hands. Then after introducing Emily, Ingrid and Raven to the deputy marshal, he said, 'Marshal's office didn't waste any time sending you here.'

Macahan shrugged. 'The mayor wired my boss soon as Sheriff Forbes resigned. I don't know what he said exactly, but it worked. I was on the next train.'

'Must be a walk in the desert compared to the gunplay you're used to in El Paso.'

Macahan smiled wryly. 'Every town has its own problems and its own personality. Same with any good lawman. Trick is findin' a way to uphold the integrity of the law without steppin' on too many toes.'

'Already a diplomat,' Drifter said, amused. Then sobering: 'Reckon you should know that Forbes is dead.'

'Comancheros?'

Drifter nodded. 'Split his skull with a machete.'

Macahan looked grim. 'Anythin' else I should know?'

'Not that I can think of.'

'How 'bout you, young lady,' Macahan said to Emily, 'you ever find your mares or the stallion?'

'No,' Drifter said, before Emily could answer. 'But we're still looking.'

'Maybe I can help you there,' Macahan said. 'If you stop by the office tomorrow and give me their description, I'll put some feelers out.'

'Thank you. I appreciate that,' Emily said. 'I would give anything to get Diablo back.'

'Diablo – that's the stallion's name?'

'Yes – well, actually it's El Diablo, but most of the time I just call him Diablo.'

Macahan nodded, and made a mental note of it.

'If you got time for a beer, I'm buying,' Drifter offered.

'Thanks. I'm meeting with the city leaders later to discuss some new town ordinances. Reckon it'd be wise

44

not to have foam on my mustache.' Tipping his hat to Ingrid and the girls, 'Ladies,' Macahan headed for the door.

'He don't look so tough,' Raven said disparagingly. 'If I was an outlaw I wouldn't be scared of him.'

'That'd be your first mistake,' Drifter said.

'And probably your last,' Ingrid added. 'Like your father always said: beware of the man who doesn't need to brag to prove himself.' She paused as the waitress arrived, served them their refreshments and left, and then said to Emily, 'I've been meaning to ask you, my dear: by any chance have we met before?'

Emily hesitated, trying to think of a way to reply without revealing her mother's infidelity, and finally looked at Drifter for help.

'Emily grew up with the Mercers,' he explained. 'That's where you probably met her.'

'Why, of course,' Ingrid exclaimed. 'Frank and Martha – how rude of me not to remember.' Pressing her hand sympathetically over Emily's, she added: 'I am so sorry for your loss, dear. I didn't know your family well, but from the few times we did meet they seemed to be warm and very giving.'

'Thank you,' Emily said. 'That's how everyone felt.'

'If you're her pa,' Raven said to Drifter, 'how come you let your daughter grow up with the Mercers?'

'Dear God,' Ingrid breathed. Then, angrily to Raven, 'One more word out of you, young lady, and I swear when we get home I'll tan your hide.'

Raven glared at her, muttered, 'Goodgodalmighty,' and fell silent.

Drifter, seeing how embarrassed Emily looked, decided to put her at ease. 'Sometimes,' he told Raven, 'even though you love someone, relationships don't work out. I was too young and restless to be a good husband or father, and being a scout for the army kept me away most of the time. So eventually Martha and I went our separate ways and she took Emily with her. That's when she met Frank Mercer and—'

'But he kept coming by the ranch to see me,' Emily interrupted, smiling gratefully at Drifter, 'didn't you, Papa?'

'As often as I could,' he said. He grasped her hand and squeezed it fondly. 'And now I'm gonna do everything I can to make up for my absence.'

Touched by Drifter's sincerity, Ingrid smiled.

Raven didn't. ''Least you got a father,' she said enviously. 'That's more'n I got!' Suddenly tears welled in her big black eyes and jumping up, she ran out.

Ingrid closed her eyes as if in pain. When she opened them again, she looked pale and miserable. 'I'm sorry she behaved so badly,' she said to Drifter and Emily. 'Raven really isn't a bad child – in fact, there's a tremendous amount of good in her. But she was terribly close to her father and right now, she misses him so much she's angry at the whole world – and especially me, it seems.'

'You?' Drifter said, frowning.

'Yes,' Ingrid said sadly. 'You see her father was shot and killed here in town… and Raven blames me for it.'

CHAPTER NINE

After saying goodbye to Ingrid and Raven, Drifter and Emily took adjoining rooms at the Carlisle Hotel and then crossed the street and stabled their horses and the pack-mule at Lars Gustafson's Livery. Gustafson was a cantankerous old Swede, hobbled by arthritis, whose ratty gray beard was stained with years of tobacco juice. He was proud of the fact that no one had ever accused him of bathing too often, yet he kept his stables spotless. He also was gentle with horses and fiercely loyal to the few men he called friends.

Drifter was one of those friends. Sheriff Lonnie Forbes had been another – though an outsider never would have guessed it. The two men argued incessantly and disagreed on everything, especially how to play checkers.

Now, as Drifter and Emily turned their horses over to Lars, Drifter noticed that the old, stained checkerboard on which the two friends always played on, was sitting on the empty beer keg near the stalls . . . its checkers set up for a new game.

Realizing that it would never be played, Drifter said: ''Fraid I got bad news for you. . . .'

'If you mean 'bout Lonnie, I already heard.'

'From who?'

'Marshal Macahan. He was just here to get a loose shoe fixed.' Gustafson grimaced and spat his disgust on the straw-strewn floor. 'Yesus, a machete ain't no way for a lawman to die.'

'I agree. But 'least it's quick,' Drifter said. 'Beats dying in bed, rotting away with some lingering fever. If that ever happens,' he added to Emily, 'I want you to promise that you'll shoot me.'

'I will do no such thing,' she declared.

'Why not? You'd shoot a horse or a dog to put it out of its misery, why not me?'

'Because this is not the Dark Ages, it is the end of the nineteenth century. New medicines are discovered every day. How do you think I would feel if I put you out of your misery, as you call it, and the next day a cure was found? Why, I would never forgive myself. I am right, aren't I?' she said when Drifter didn't reply. 'Admit it.'

'I'm admitting nothing,' Drifter grumbled. 'Now c'mon . . . let's get back to the hotel. We can both use a bath.'

Gustafson stopped them, 'Wait,' he said. 'There's somethin' you oughta know.'

'Like what?'

The old hostler hesitated, uneasy about what he was about to say, then told Emily, 'I don't usually go stickin' my nose into other folks' business, but I liked your pa. Liked him a whole heap. In my book Frank Mercer was a fine church-goin' man an' I hate to see you get took advantage of—'

'What're you talking about?' Drifter cut in.

'Miss Emily's stallion.'

'What about him?' she said.

'Well, somehow, while you two was huntin' them Comancheros in Mexico, Stadtlander got his hands on him.'

'Mr Stadtlander has Diablo?' Emily said, shocked.

'Yup. His boy, Slade an' the Iverson brothers were in town this mornin', braggin' about him. Said El Diablo was twice the stud Brandy was – you know, that black Morgan stallion Gabe Moonlight stole from him?'

Emily waited until she and Drifter were a few steps from the livery stable before pulling him aside and insisting: 'We have to ride out and see Mr Stadtlander right away.'

'Tonight?'

' 'Course tonight.'

'And do what?'

'Get Diablo back.'

'And just how do you expect to do that – by asking him?' Mimicking her voice, he added, 'Oh by the way, Mr Stadtlander, I have just found out you have my prize stallion. I've no idea how you got hold of him, but I'd like him back, *por favor.*'

'There is no need to be sarcastic,' Emily said. 'I am not a child.'

'Then stop acting like one. Look,' Drifter continued, softening, 'I know how much that horse means to you, and I know the sooner he's yours again the happier you'll be—'

'Then?'

'But I also know Stillman J. Stadtlander! He's a tough, ruthless, greedy sonofabitch who will stop at nothing to get what he wants, and that includes murder. Judas, Emily, look what he did to Gabe for beating him at poker – branded him a horse-thief, bribed the law to throw a rope over him, offered a huge reward to anyone who brought Gabe in – dead or alive. I mean, does that sound like a man willing to hand over a stallion worth thousands of dollars – a stallion, oh by the way, that he probably stole in the first place – to a fifteen-year-old girl who has no bill of sale saying the horse is hers?'

'But it is not just me saying it,' Emily protested. 'Everyone in Santa Rosa knows that El Diablo belonged to us.'

'Yeah, and not one of those brave souls will step forward and admit it for fear of getting on Stadtlander's wrong side.'

'I don't care,' Emily said stubbornly. 'Diablo's mine and I want him back.'

'And you'll get him back, that's a promise. But only if you're patient and willing to do it legal and right.'

' 'Mean hire a lawyer . . . go to court?'

'If necessary, yes. But first let's talk to the marshal. See if he's willing to ride out to the Double S with us tomorrow morning and find out just how Stadtlander got his hands on the stallion in the first place.'

'What good is that going to do? Mr Stadtlander controls all the law in New Mexico.'

'He doesn't *control* Ezra Macahan. Of that I assure you. Macahan's a stickler for obeying the law and his integrity isn't for sale – not even to the mighty Stillman J. Stadtlander!'

'Fine!' Emily said angrily. 'We will do it your way. But I warn you, if I cannot get Diablo back the legal way, I will get him back my way – and that may not be so legal!'

CHAPTER TEN

The next morning after a quick breakfast at the hotel, they went to the sheriff's office. It felt strange not to find Lonnie Forbes dozing behind his desk, long legs propped up on the desk, and for a moment Drifter and Emily felt a twinge of sadness.

The office was empty but a scraggly Mexican boy mopping the jail cells told them that Deputy Macahan had ridden off earlier.

'*Sabe donde fue el Mariscal?*' Drifter asked.

'*Sí, señor. Para hablar con el Señor Stadtlander.*'

'*Muchas gracias.*' Drifter flipped a quarter to the boy. Then he and Emily left and walked over to the livery stable. There, as Gustafson brought out their horses, Emily asked Drifter if he thought it was merely a coincidence that Macahan had gone to talk to Stadtlander?

Drifter shrugged. 'What else could it be?'

'Well, could be he went there deliberately to warn him that we are looking for Diablo.'

' 'Mean so he could hide him from you?'

'Maybe.'

'You're getting your lawmen mixed up,' Drifter said. 'Forbes might have done something like that but not Macahan. Like I told you yesterday, his integrity ain't for sale.'

Stillman J. Stadtlander's cattle ranch, the Double S, consisted of 200,000 acres. The ranch was not one single contiguous parcel of land, but rather six immense sections that Stadtlander had acquired over twenty years by finding ways to force the original owners to sell at a loss. Each section had only one common border with another, in most cases the connecting land so small the sections resembled individual islands that when lumped together encompassed 315 square miles.

It was an hour's ride from Santa Rosa to the high, arched, signature gateway that warned everyone they were entering Double S land; and then another twenty minute climb up to the crest of the flat-topped knoll on which stood Stadtlander's large, impressive, Western-style mansion. Originally, Stadtlander had built his home atop the low grassy hill so he could defend himself against any Indian attacks; then later, when the tribes were confined to reservations, and he could afford it, he replaced his modest single-story ranch house with a fancy three-story mansion to let everyone know how rich and important he'd become.

Now as Drifter and Emily rode up the long grassy incline, Emily asked her father if he'd ever been here before. He nodded and explained that four years ago Stadtlander's foreman had hired him to break a bunch of wild mustangs that had been rounded up. 'I'd heard stories about Stadtlander from other hands who'd worked for him, most of them griping about how hard he pushed them, but what the hell, I needed to eat, the wages were fair and the grub plentiful and with thirty broomtails to break I figured I could count on at least six weeks' steady work.'

'What happened?' Emily asked as Drifter paused.

'I butted heads with the Iverson brothers. Mace and Cody got a big laugh out of bullying new hands, especially young fellas fresh to cowboying; and one morning, after I'd been there about two weeks, I got tired of them picking on this kid just up from Laredo and told them to back off. I didn't know it at the time but the Iversons were drinking pals of Stadlander's boy, Slade, and that night the three of them braced me while we were all washing up for supper. I didn't want any trouble, or to lose my job but I couldn't back down, 'cause I knew if I did they'd never quit jerking my tail, so I told them to slap leather or go about their business.'

'Did they draw on you?'

'The Iversons didn't – they don't have the sand for a face-down. Slade isn't much better but he, like me, knew he'd been backed into a corner – draw and he might be killed, not draw and he'd lose the respect of the men. At the same time I knew if I shot the boss's son, I'd find myself dancing from the end of a rope.' Drifter paused and shook his head. 'I tell you, it was a real Mexican stand-off.'

They rode on up the slope in silence. The sun felt

hot on their necks and the dry, windless air was alive with jumping grasshoppers. Emily kept waiting for her father to continue but he never said a word. Finally, as they neared the top of the hill Emily lost her patience. 'Well, go on. Finish your story. What happened?'

'Your favorite outlaw, Gabe, showed up.'

'Gabe – what does he have to do with it?'

'Everything. He worked for Stadtlander at the time as his top gun. He'd been in the house talking to the old man when Slade and the Iversons braced me, but fortunately for me, he came up right as I was waiting for Slade to make his play and stepped between us. "Quint", he said to me, "go eat. An' you", he told Slade, "go talk to your daddy".

' "Don't tell me what to do", Slade barked. "You work for me, remember?"

' "I work for your father", Gabe corrected. "An' he just told me to go find you an' tell you he wants to talk to you. End of conversation". Turning to the hands who'd gathered around us, he added, "Show's over. Get to eatin' ".

'And that was it. Later I thanked Gabe for what he'd done and he grinned and said, "Don't thank me yet, *amigo*. Just 'cause you walked away without havin' to jerk your iron don't mean it's over 'tween you'n Slade. Or the Iversons. They're meaner than blind weasels, all three of 'em. An' they ain't gonna let you get away with callin' them out in front of a bunch of waddies".

' "You sayin' I should pick up my wages?"

' "You've had worse ideas". So that's what I did. Ain't been back since.'

Drifter stopped talking as he and Emily reached the crest of the hill. They reined in their horses to give them a brief blow and then continued on at a walk. The land leveled out, flat as a tabletop. Ahead of them a white, three-barred fence enclosed the various corrals and outer buildings that surrounded the main ranch house. Several hands were painting the bunkhouse; others repairing the roof of the barn. Their hammering echoed about the property, hiding all the other noises that were being made by men going about their daily chores.

Drifter and Emily rode through the open gate and across the big yard fronting the huge, multi-leveled gray house. A covered, shady porch ran around the entire building. A lone horse was tied up at the hitch-rail. As they reined up beside it and dismounted, Emily glanced around for her stallion. But El Diablo was not in any of the corrals and she guessed Stadtlander had the horse hidden somewhere.

Just then the front door opened and a small, wiry, well-dressed gunman with blond curly hair stepped out.

'Hidee, Quint . . . Miss Emily,' Latigo said, smiling. 'Come on in. Mr Stadtlander's expectin' you.'

CHAPTER ELEVEN

Stadtlander's study occupied one whole corner of the mansion. Two walls of the huge oak-paneled room were adorned with paintings depicting western scenes: Custer's Last Stand; a herd of stampeding cattle; a trail drive; a cowboy riding a bucking mustang; Comanches attacking a wagon train – every picture vividly showed a slice of daily life on the range. The other two walls were broken up by windows, one side facing the seemingly endless scrubland on which a vast herd of beef cattle grazed and the other offering a panoramic view of the valley floor all the way to the distant Rio Grande.

The massive furniture was covered in brown-and-white cowhide and the stone fireplace was big enough to spit-roast a whole steer. Above it hung an imposing portrait of Stadtlander astride a magnificent black Morgan (the same stallion he had accused Gabriel Moonlight of stealing), while facing him across the room was an equally impressive painting of his deceased wife, Agatha. A pale, delicate, sweet-faced Easterner of obvious fine breeding, she seemed out of place in this heady, macho-filled atmosphere.

Hanging beside her, one on either side, were smaller portraits of their children, Slade and his dead sister, Elizabeth, both in their early teens.

Stadtlander and Deputy US Marshal Macahan sat talking in front of the paintings. It was a testy conversation. The ageing, jut-jawed rancher objected to reprimands from anyone – especially a lanky, laconic lawman young enough to be his grandson!

Macahan had ridden out to warn him that if his son, Slade, and his pals, the Iverson brothers, didn't curb their wild drinking and brawling sprees along Lower Front Street, then he would have no choice but to arrest them.

'You do,' Stadtlander warned, 'and you'll be wastin' good taxpayers' money. My lawyer will have them boys out almost 'fore you can lock the jail door. What's more, there ain't a circuit judge in the territory that's gonna do more than fine 'em a few measly dollars for fear of buckin' me.'

'So what I'm hearin' is,' Macahan said softly, 'you're expectin' me to turn a blind eye when they shoot up the town?'

'Why not? Like all my hands, they work hard every day so who can blame 'em if they ride into town now an' then to have a little fun. It's only natural. 'Sides, I always pay for any damages. So what's to complain about? Anyway, why should you care? You're just here temporarily, castin' an empty shadow till a new sheriff gets voted in. An' when the day comes to count the votes, you can bet I'll have plenty to say about who gets elected . . . an' who don't.'

'In other words, you're callin' the shots?'

'Damn right I am! Without my money an' my influence, Santa Rosa would still be a mud hole in the desert. So it's only right an' fair that I make the rules.'

Macahan said quietly, 'That mean you're above the law?'

'Never said that,' Stadtlander argued. 'So don't go puttin' words in my mouth.' He glowered, trying to stare down Macahan. But the young deputy refused to be intimidated by the short, white-haired, pugnacious rancher who, now in his seventies and afflicted with gout, couldn't walk without a cane. And before they could continue their war of words, there was a knock and the door opened.

Both men rose as Drifter and Emily were ushered in by Latigo. The little gunfighter seemed more truculent than ever. He walked with an arrogant swagger and his faintly sneering smile suggested that although he was willing to take Stadtlander's money, he was neither intimidated nor impressed by the rancher's display of pompous, self-importance.

'Reckon you folks all know each other,' he drawled. 'So I'll skip the introductions.'

Stadtlander forced himself to smile. But he couldn't disguise his displeasure as he told the little Texan to, 'Send Chang in.' Waiting until Latigo left, he then stepped forward and, ignoring Drifter, greeted Emily. 'It's a pleasure to see you again, Miss Mercer. I don't know if you remember or not, but you and your pa once came here to talk to me—'

'I remember,' Emily said. 'You came out to our ranch once, too.'

'Indeed I did,' Stadtlander said. 'You have a good memory, little lady. By the way, though I was away and could not come to the funeral, let me say how mighty saddened I am by your tragic loss. Your family was admired and loved by all of us, and with their passing Santa Rosa has lost some of its finest citizens.'

It sounded like a politician's speech and Drifter had a hard time swallowing it. But Emily managed to say politely: 'Thank you, sir. I'm sure they would be happy to know that.'

A white-jacketed Chinese manservant shuffled in and bowed politely to Stadtlander, who turned to Emily.

'May I offer you somethin' cool to drink, Miss Mercer? Chang, here, rustles up some mighty tasty lemonade.'

Emily nodded, 'Lemonade would be fine,' and then asked Drifter, 'Would you care for some?'

Knowing it would annoy Stadtlander, Drifter nodded. 'Sure.'

'Make that four glasses,' Stadtlander told Chang.

The Chinaman bowed and exited.

Stadtlander indicated the couch. 'Please, be seated. Now,' he said when they were comfortable, 'Why don't you tell me what your visit is about?'

Again, he spoke directly to Emily, who said innocently, 'I have come for my horse, El Diablo.'

There was a tense silence during which all the air seemed to have been sucked out of the room.

Drifter watched Stadtlander intently. The defiant old

rancher's eyes flicked in the direction of Macahan, who sat impassive as a bronze statue, then returned to Emily, locking on her unflinching, wide-eyed gaze.

'Yes,' he said after a long pause, 'of course. I was expectin' you in fact.' He cleared his throat and leaned forward, both hands pressed on top of his cane. 'Unfortunately, the stallion is no longer yours.'

'What do you mean?'

Stadtlander rose, limped to a desk, took a document from a drawer, returned and handed it to Emily. 'As you can see,' he said as she scanned the contents. 'This is a bill of sale, legally signed by the registered owner of the stallion—'

'He is a liar!' Emily snapped. 'Nobody owned him but me.'

'Easy . . .' Drifter murmured.

Stadtlander smiled, the smile of a poker player who has just been dealt a royal flush, and said to Emily, 'Naturally, you have proof of ownership?'

'I do not need proof. Everyone within five hundred miles of here knows my dad' – she broke off and eyed Drifter, who nodded to show he understood her reluctance to admit he was her father – 'bought Diablo at a horse auction in El Paso. I know. I was with him.'

'Lots of people buy lots of things, Miss Mercer. But that don't mean they keep them forever; especially if there's a profit to be made by sellin' them.'

'Father would never have sold Diablo – not for any amount of profit. What would be the point? With no stallion to breed with our mares, there would be no foals to sell and the ranch would have gone under.'

'Well, be that as it may,' Stadtlander said. 'Sell the horse he did, as Mr Foster's signature at the bottom of that document proves. So I'm afraid—'

Drifter cut him off. 'Where's this Foster now?'

'In his office in Deming.'

'That doesn't sound like a guess,' Drifter said. 'By any chance does he work for you?'

'He does now,' Stadtlander admitted. 'But he didn't when he sold me the stallion.'

Drifter snorted and looked at Macahan. 'That's mighty convenient, wouldn't you say, Ezra?'

Macahan turned to Stadtlander. 'Any particular reason you suddenly decided to hire this fella?'

'It wasn't done *suddenly*, Deputy. I've had my eye on Luke Foster for some time now. I've long been unhappy with the man who represents me at the auctions, so when Foster came to me with the stallion, I liked his brass an' asked him if he'd like to go to work for me . . . an' he said yes. Simple as that.'

Macahan nodded, satisfied with the explanation.

Drifter said, 'This sale, Mr Stadtlander – when'd it take place?'

'Exactly three days after Frank Mercer and his family were killed. You can check the date at the top of the page for verification.'

'I don't need to check anything,' Drifter said. He included Macahan as he added, 'I was there at the ranch, with the Mercers, when the Comancheros attacked. The stallion was still in the barn and Frank was willing to risk his life to go get it and bring it back to the house—'

'I find that hard to believe,' Stadtlander said, 'considerin' his gout was even worse than mine.'

'That's why I went for him,' Drifter said.

'You risked your life for strangers?' Macahan questioned.

'The Mercers weren't strangers. I'd known them for years.'

'And you managed to save the stallion?'

Drifter ducked the question. 'I made it to the barn and started to take him out of the stall when I was jumped by two Comancheros. One of them cold-cocked me. When I came to, the Mercers were dead and the Comancheros were gone. So were all the horses—'

'Then you didn't save the stallion?'

'No. But during the whole time I was with the Mercers, before and during the attack, Frank never once mentioned selling El Diablo. It was just the opposite in fact: he was all fired up about how much money he was going to make from stud fees and the foals his mares were going to drop next spring.'

'Would you be willin' to swear to that?' Macahan asked.

'Before any judge in the territory.'

'An' all that stuff that happened in the barn – will you swear to that too?'

'He don't have to,' Stadtlander assured the lawman. 'He's tellin' the truth.'

'How do you know that?'

'I talked to Lieutenant James Ellesworth, whose patrol found Mr Longley. He showed me his written report. It clearly states Longley was wanderin' around outside the barn, bleedin' from a head wound. Which only confirms,' Stadtlander added smugly, 'Mr Foster's story.'

'What story is that, sir?'

'That, like I said, he bought the stallion from Frank Mercer exactly one week before the massacre.'

'Then how come the horse was still there when the Comancheros hit us?' Drifter said.

'Under normal conditions it wouldn't have been. Mr Foster paid cash for the horse and would've taken it with him. But due to an important horse auction in El Paso – an auction he'd already planned to attend – he asked Frank to hold El Diablo for him until he returned. Since it was only for a few days, Frank agreed. But of course, unfortunately by the time Mr Foster did return, the Mercers were dead and the stallion . . . gone.'

'So how'd he get his hands on it again?' Macahan asked.

'Ah-h,' said Stadtlander, 'therein lies a true miracle: as he was ridin' to Deming, he happened to see the stallion runnin' loose in the foothills and managed to lay a rope on him—'

'Running-loose-be-damned!' Drifter said angrily. 'Way that horse can carry the mail, once he got free ain't no one could rope him.'

'Meanin'?'

'Your man Foster either stole the goddamn horse or bought it from the Comancheros!'

'Either way Diablo was never legally his to sell,'

chimed in Emily.

Unruffled, Stadtlander said, 'I can understand your feelings, Miss Mercer. But as I'm sure Deputy Macahan, here, will agree – that document in your hands says differently.' He reached out and took the bill of sale back from Emily. 'The stallion is legally mine and I intend to keep him.'

'We will see about that,' she said, rising.

The three men rose with her.

Macahan said quietly, 'I don't know what you plan to do next, Miss Mercer. But whatever it is, make sure it's within the law. I wouldn't want to have to arrest you.'

'I would not want that either,' Emily said sweetly. 'But thank you for your advice anyway.' Turning to Drifter, she added, 'We have to get back to Santa Rosa. There is a train leaving this afternoon for Las Cruces. I want to be on it.'

'Why? What's in Las Cruces?'

'An attorney I know.' She went to the door, paused and looked back at the stoop-shouldered, white-haired rancher. 'See you in court, Mr Stadtlander.'

CHAPTER TWELVE

'Do you really know a lawyer in Las Cruces?' Drifter asked Emily as they stepped off the porch and walked to their horses, 'or was that just for Stadtlander's benefit?'

She started to answer then stopped as she saw Latigo approaching from the barn. With him was Stadtlander's son. Slade was taller and leaner than his father but possessed none of the older man's pride or indomitable spirit. He also had a mean streak the Marquis de Sade would have envied.

'Hey, Quint!' Latigo yelled.

Drifter stopped and with Emily waited for Latigo and Slade to join them.

'Get things straightened out?' Latigo asked Emily, his voice as mocking as his smile.

'Mr Stadtlander made it perfectly clear that he has no intention of giving me my horse,' she replied. 'If that is what you mean?'

'That's 'cause El Diablo ain't your horse,' Slade said. His voice, though low and manly, had a whine to it that suggested he'd been badly spoiled. 'Pa bought him, fair'n square from a horse-trader.'

'Your pa,' Drifter said, slow and deliberate, 'never did anything fair and square in his entire miserable life.'

Slade stiffened and his right hand hovered over the Colt holstered on his hip.

'Gonna make you eat those words,' he told Drifter.

'Emily,' Drifter said, eyes never leaving Slade, 'move away from me.'

'No need for that,' Latigo said, moving between them. 'Be no shootin' here today.'

'He's right,' Stadtlander said, limping out on to the porch. 'You two,' he added to Drifter and Emily. 'You've spoke your piece: you got your answer. Now, mount up an' get the hell off my property.'

'Sounds like good advice,' Macahan said. He stepped off the porch and joined Drifter and Emily. 'I can use some company back to town anyway.'

Drifter hesitated, eyes fixed on Slade. Peripherally, he saw that Latigo was poised to draw. Knowing this was one fight he could only lose, he nodded to Emily to continue and together they walked to their horses.

Macahan looked hard and long at Latigo. 'I've heard of you, Rawlins.'

'What've you heard?'

'You're fast.'

Latigo smiled his little sneering smile and his amber eyes became menacing slits. 'Anythin' else?'

'Rest is just rumors.'

'Name one.'

'Well, I don't hold much stock in rumors, but I heard

you got paid to go to Chihuahua to kill some Mexican ranchers.' He eyed Stadtlander accusingly before adding, 'Ranchers whose land was on both sides of the border – land that a certain person wanted for themselves.'

On the porch Stadtlander reddened angrily. 'You referrin' to me, Deputy?'

Macahan said, 'I don't know, Mr Stadtlander. Am I?'

Stadtlander reddened even more.

'Goddammit!' Slade snarled at Latigo. 'You just gonna stand there an' let this no-good sidewinder talk 'bout my pa like that?'

'I don't kill deputy US marshals,' Latigo said, smirking. 'I got too much respect for the law.' Tipping his hat to Emily he said, 'Good day, miss,' and walked back to the barn.

Stadtlander, veins threatening to pop in his forehead, glared at Macahan. 'Lawman or not, you ever accuse me again of payin' to have folks killed, I'll shoot you myself!' Leaning heavily on his cane, he stormed back into the house.

'An' if'n he don't,' Slade warned Macahan, 'I will.'

Macahan's right hand, balled into a fist, came up swiftly from his side and slammed into Slade's jaw. The younger Stadtlander crumpled like a felled tree. Standing over him, Macahan said grimly, 'Next time you threaten me, chuck-a-luck, you're gonna wake up in jail.' Moving to his horse, he stepped into the saddle and looked at Drifter and Emily.

' 'Less you got other business here, reckon we should ride.'

Drifter looked questioningly at Emily. 'No,' she said. 'I think we are done here.'

The three of them rode out through the gate ... watched by the angry eyes of the hands looking on.

CHAPTER THIRTEEN

They hadn't ridden far when Emily suddenly reined up her horse. Caught off-guard, Drifter and Macahan rode on for a few steps before stopping and turning back to her.

'What's wrong?' Drifter asked.

'I have to ask you something,' she said to Macahan. 'It is about Latigo.'

'I'm listenin'.'

'When Quint and I first saw him in Mexico, it was near the border and he was pinned down by several Mexicans. He told Quint that they were *bandidos*—'

'Said they'd jumped him not far from where we found him,' Drifter added.

'Go on,' Macahan said.

'What I want to know is,' Emily continued, 'these rumors about Latigo being hired to kill those ranchers – do you think they are true?'

'If I knew the answer to that, Miss Mercer, I wouldn't have called them rumors. I will say this though – accordin' to the wire I received this mornin' from the

Marshal in El Paso, several important ranchers in Chihuahua are hollerin' for us to arrest Latigo for murder – Latigo *and* anyone who was with him.'

'That'd be me,' Drifter said.

'Us,' Emily corrected.

'You helped him shoot those men?'

'Yeah – but only after they shot at me,' Drifter said. He went on to explain what happened.

'They sure acted like *bandidos*,' Emily said. 'I mean what kind of ranchers, Mexican or American, hide in bushes and shoot at strangers?'

'Ones whose neighbors were bushwhacked – picked off one by one from a long way off by an expert rifle-man—'

'—armed, I'll bet, with a Sharps-Borchardt rifle using a telescope for a sight.'

'How do you know that?'

Drifter said only, 'Damn! After all these years you'd think I'd know better than to trust that sonofabitch.'

'It is still only a rumor,' Emily reminded.

'Not to the widows of the husbands they just buried,' Macahan said grimly.

Stung, Emily looked away and chewed her lip.

'What're you gonna do?' Drifter asked Macahan.

The lawman shrugged his wide, rawboned shoulders. 'Nothin' I can do. Marshal's office has no jurisdiction in Mexico. Wants none neither. Rawlins could kill a hundred men an' so long as he does it south of the border, my orders are to leave it strictly up to the *rurales*.'

'What about Stadtlander?' Emily asked. 'If those

71

rumors are right, he is just as responsible for killing those ranchers as Latigo is.'

'Give me proof to back that up,' Macahan said, 'an' I'll arrest him as an accessory to murder. Otherwise he's free as a jay bird, like always.' Removing his Stetson he wiped the sweat from his forehead and the leather hatband inside, then replaced the hat and nudged his horse forward.

Emily started to follow him. But Drifter grabbed her reins, saying: 'You never answered my question: do you really know a lawyer in Las Cruces who might help you get your horse back?'

'No,' she said. 'That was just for Mr Stadtlander's benefit, like you said. But that does not mean to say that I am giving up. I'm going to get El Diablo back if it takes me the rest of my life.'

CHAPTER FOURTEEN

A mile or so before they reached Santa Rosa, Drifter and Emily said goodbye to Macahan and turned southwest on to the trail leading to her ranch. It was less than an hour's ride and Drifter, still angered by Latigo's lies and the fact that he'd been tricked into killing several innocent Mexican ranchers, barely spoke a word to Emily. She made a few attempts to start a conversation; then, when his only response was a surly grunt, she gave up and concentrated on her own thoughts.

She really only had one thought of importance: how to legally recover El Diablo. First, she obviously needed to hire an attorney. But how could she hire one when she had little or no money with which to pay him? Equally depressing, even if she sold the ranch and used that money for attorney fees, the chances of finding a lawyer willing to go up against Stillman J. Stadtlander were remote and . . . nil.

Yet she could not just give up. Not and live with

herself. Defeat wasn't acceptable. Like her mother before her, Emily believed that failure was not the missing of success, but the giving up of trying. And by God, like she'd just told Drifter, she was never going to give up.

She was abruptly jolted out of her reverie by her horse. Startled by a family of Gambel's Quail darting in front of it, their comma-shaped topknots waving as they ran, the pale-colored dun skittered sideways almost unseating her. She grabbed its dark mane with one hand, the saddle horn with the other, and clung on until the horse calmed down. It was then she looked ahead and realized she was almost home. She nudged her horse forward, following the winding trail as it narrowed and descended between rocks and clumps of ocotillo to the little valley in which sat her ranch.

It was the first time she had been home since her family had been killed, and as she rode in front of Drifter, the sight of the squat, rock-walled, log-roofed ranch-house brought a thousand memories flooding back to her. It also reminded her that she would never see her family again. The finality of that realization swept over her like a shroud of gloom, adding to her depression.

'Maybe I have made a mistake coming here,' she said, looking back at Drifter. 'Maybe we should turn around and go back to town.'

'Your call,' he said, shrugging. 'But if it was me, I'd want to sleep on it first.'

'But that is the point,' she said. 'I don't know if I can spend the night here. Or want to.'

74

'Fair enough.'

They rode on in silence. It was almost dusk. Insects whined about their heads. At last the trail flattened out and stretched across a flat, sparsely-grassed area that ended at the three-barred fence enclosing the house, barn, and corrals. Empty corrals, she noted sadly, as they rode in through the gate. Empty corrals. Empty barn. Empty house. Empty *everything*!

The dun came to a stop and patiently stood there in the fading light. Emily realized they had reached the hitching rail fronting the house. Dismounting, she and Drifter tied up their horses and walked to the porch.

But when she reached there, her legs suddenly froze and she couldn't go any farther. 'I cannot do it,' she told Drifter.

'Sure you can.'

'No. You do not understand. I cannot go in there. I won't. . . .'

'Maybe if I wait out here... and you go in alone. . . .'

'No.' She shook her head adamantly. 'I want to go back to town.'

Drifter signed wearily. 'OK. But I want to warn you: if you do that . . . if you run away without going in there and facing down these demons . . . you'll regret it for the rest of your life.'

'You don't know that. You are just saying it to get me to go in.'

'No,' he said gently. 'I do know that – from personal experience.'

'Your folks were killed?'

He nodded.

She studied him suspiciously. 'Serious?'

'Serious.'

'When? How?'

'When I was thirteen. My dad was a whiskey salesman whose territory was the whole South-west. He was gone a lot and sometimes, if where he was going wasn't too far away, Mother left me with her sister and went with him.'

'What happened?'

'One day they didn't come home.' Drifter paused, and for a moment his fierce gray eyes clouded with sadness, then, 'Apache renegades attacked their stage out of Bisbee. When it didn't show up at the relay station, the soldiers went looking for it. It took a while but they finally found it not far from the trail. It was still burning and everyone was dead. They found all the bodies but . . . never did find their scalps.'

Emily paled. 'I-I'm so sorry, Quint. I did not know.'

'How could you? I never told anyone. Not even your mother.'

'And you didn't go back to your house?'

'Never. Never even went to the funeral. My aunt and uncle tried to make me go but I ran off . . . stole a horse and kept riding till . . . I couldn't ride anymore.'

He stopped talking. Emily waited for him to continue. When he didn't, she thought for several moments before asking, 'Do you think you would have been different if you had gone to the funeral?'

Drifter shrugged. 'I don't know. But I've always thought that perhaps by seeing them, you know, in their graves, I would have been forced to accept that

76

they were really dead. Then I could have gotten on with my life . . . maybe even married and settled down, had a family that I was willing to raise and look after . . . instead of just drifting around, refusing to grow any roots.'

There was a silence save for the early-evening crickets chirping in the grass and the distant *ka-KAA-kaaing* of quail out in the scrubland.

Then Emily gave a determined little smile and said to Drifter, 'Well, now you have me.'

'We have each other,' he corrected.

She nodded and offered him her hand. 'Let us go inside,' she said.

He took her hand. It felt soft and cool and perfect.

Emily gripped her father's calloused hand tightly. It felt strong and comforting and perfect.

Together they climbed on to the porch and entered the house.

CHAPTER FIFTEEN

Inside, Drifter lit the kerosene lamp that lay on its side on the supper table. By its warm yellow light the living area looked much the same as he remembered it the last time he had been there: windows broken, furniture overturned, blood spilled on the floor where the bodies had lain.

And everywhere . . . there was the smell of death.

Lieutenant Ellesworth, the officer in charge of the patrol, had been with him then. After verifying that Frank Mercer, his wife Martha and two sons were dead and brutally scalped, the lieutenant called in several troopers and ordered them to carry the bodies outside to be buried.

' 'Fore you do that,' Drifter said grimly, 'you should know there's another young'un, a daughter named Emily.'

'Where is she?'

'At boarding school in Las Cruces.'

'Know her pretty well, do you?'

'Well enough to know she'd want to be here when

her family was buried.'

'Somebody's gonna have to wire her – tell her what happened.'

'I will,' Drifter said.

Lieutenant Ellesworth considered briefly before saying, 'So be it.' He then told the troopers to put the corpses in a wagon so they could be taken to Santa Rosa.

Now, as Drifter looked at Emily standing beside him, he marveled at how well she had managed to control her emotions. Few adults could have done as well.

'I need to know something,' she said after looking around.

'Ask.'

'The bloodstains,' she pointed. 'Which one belongs to Momma? Please,' she said, as he hesitated, 'I want to know where she died. I want to know where everyone was when they died.'

'That may not be a good idea.'

'Please.'

'All right,' Drifter agreed reluctantly. Indicating each bloodstain as he spoke, he said, 'Your mom was there . . . Frank, there . . . and . . . those two, that's where your brothers stood.'

Emily closed her eyes as if committing everything to memory. Then she took a deep breath, trying to calm herself. She was silent for several moments. Then she said: 'You were not with them when they – it happened, were you?'

'No, I was in the barn.'

'To rescue Diablo, according to Sheriff Forbes.'

'That's right. Frank said he could live with losing the mares, just so the stallion wasn't stolen. He wanted to go himself, but because of his gout he couldn't run, so I went instead. He and your brothers kept the Comancheros pinned down and I was able to reach the barn and get inside OK, but two of them were already in there. One hit me from behind and. . . that's all I remember till the soldiers showed up.'

'So you do not know if Momma or the others suffered or. . . .' Her voice cracked and she turned away so he wouldn't see her tears.

'They didn't,' he lied. 'That I know for sure.'

'But if you weren't—'

'By their expressions . . . way they were lying . . . as peaceful as if they'd just gone to sleep. I knew then that they were all dead by the time they were scalped, and Lieutenant Ellesworth agreed with me.' It was another lie but Drifter deemed it necessary. Nothing good could come from telling a fifteen-year-old girl that by all appearances, and the agonized expressions frozen on their faces, her loved ones had been horribly mutilated while still alive.

'Thank God for small mercies,' Emily said. She inhaled deeply and let the air out slowly, releasing much of her pain. Then pulling herself together, she dried her eyes on her sleeve and stood straighter. 'Well,' she said, determined, 'first thing we must do is get rid of these bloodstains. Will you go draw some water while I try to light the stove?'

Drifter nodded, 'Sure,' and left, thinking that he had never been more proud of anyone.

80

CHAPTER SIXTEEN

A rooster triumphantly crowing on a corral fence awoke Drifter the next morning. It was barely dawn but already he could smell coffee and beans cooking. Surprised, he swung his legs over the side of the cot, pulled on his jeans, boots and shirt and wandered into the living-room-kitchen area – and found Emily, dressed, hair pulled back like her mother always wore hers, cracking eggs into a bowl on the table.

'You're up early,' he said, joining her.

'Couldn't sleep.' She indicated the coffee pot on the stove beside a kettle of bubbling beans. 'Help yourself. Oh, and pour me a cup, will you, please?'

He did as she asked; then stood beside her, sipping his coffee, as she poured the eggs into a black iron skillet pan that crackled with hot grease.

'Where'd you find the eggs?'

'Under some hay in the barn. When I first heard the rooster, I knew the hens were probably still around, so I went in there and looked. Beans I found in the pantry. There is a whole bunch of canned food there. And a sack of flour, too.'

'All the comforts of home,' he said without thinking.

If she heard him, she didn't show it. 'It should last us a few days and by then I will be ready to go back to school.'

He knew that was the best thing for her, but he couldn't help feeling saddened by the thought. 'Will you be selling the ranch?'

'Soon as I can find a buyer – unless you want it?'

'Uh-uh.'

'I didn't think so.' She used the spatula to splash grease over the sizzling eggs. 'As for myself, there is not much point in owning a horse ranch when you don't have any horses . . . or the money to buy them with.'

'Whoa . . . I told you I'd be happy to round up some broomtails. Might even find a stallion or two. They wouldn't have the bloodlines El Diablo has but, if we're lucky, might be they're good enough to sire some fine-looking colts. Also,' Drifter added, 'I could most likely talk Gabe into letting you use the Morgan for stud. Its bloodlines go way back . . . maybe even further than your stallion.'

Emily didn't answer right away. Then she looked sideways at him, a look that was both curious and questioning. 'That what you want me to do – stay here and raise horses?'

'N-No, I . . .it was just a suggestion.'

Then, as she made a sound that could have meant anything, 'No. Definitely not. I want you to finish school.'

'If I did stay,' she said, as if he hadn't spoken, 'would

you be staying too – helping me?'

'Only if you wanted me to.'

'No, no,' she said almost crossly, 'you are not putting all this on me. I am only fifteen, remember? You are the adult. Act like it. Don't be asking me to decide your life for you. I am having enough trouble making my own decisions.'

'I wasn't asking you to—'

'Yes-you-were,' she said. 'So stop denying it. Time to belly up to the bar, as Pa Mercer used to say. So how about it?' she said, when he didn't reply. 'As my father and only living relative, do you want me to stay or not?'

Put that way he had no trouble answering. 'I'd like you stay, Emily. And I'd like to stay here with you and raise fine horses.'

'But?'

'I want you to finish school first.'

'If I did – do – will I ever see you again?'

'As much as you want.'

'You mean after each time you come home from months of drifting?'

'I mean,' he said gently, 'every month, every week, every day if you want. And in case you're wondering how I plan on doing that let me set you straight – I intend to find work in or close to Las Cruces.'

Her lovely dark eyes became saucers. '*Truly?*'

'Truly.'

'Oh boy,' she said. 'Oh-boy-oh-boy!' Removing the skillet from the fire, she set it on the table. Then wrapping her arms around him, she hugged him so hard, he had trouble breathing.

'T-Take it easy,' he said, hugging her back. 'You're gonna crack my ribs.'

'Good,' Emily said joyfully. 'Considering all the hugs I have missed out on, you deserve to have your ribs cracked.'

They spent the next two days making the ranch look presentable, hoping to tempt potential buyers. Drifter repaired the barn door, which was hanging on one hinge, and whitewashed the corral fences and the windmill next to the well, while Emily washed the linen, curtains and their trail-soiled clothes, and swept out the house.

By sundown of the second day both were exhausted.

'I will miss this place,' Emily said as they sat on the front porch watching the sun dip below the distant mountains.

'Me too,' Drifter said, adding: 'Maybe you should reconsider selling it – or at least right now. You have enough money for schooling and if you ever run short and need something, like books or clothes or anything, I can always kick in the difference.'

Emily thought about it for moment and then shook her head. Brushing away an insect buzzing near her ear, she said, 'No. I have made up my mind. It is time to get away from all these memories and make a fresh start.'

'Memories are up here,' Drifter said, pointing at his head. 'They go wherever you go. Hard to shake 'em loose.'

'Maybe,' she admitted, 'but I am hoping that after a while I will be able to push them out of my mind with new, happier memories—' She broke off as she and Drifter heard the sound of a horse approaching. Shading their eyes against the setting sun, they saw a rider galloping across the open scrubland toward them.

CHAPTER SEVENTEEN

As the rider came closer they realized it was Raven. She looked windblown and upset and her horse was heavily lathered from galloping.

Concerned, Drifter and Emily stepped off the porch to meet her.

Like a Pony Express rider, she leapt from the saddle before the horse had stopped and came running up to them.

'Easy . . . easy . . . Calm down,' Drifter said as she started blurting out words to him. 'Take a deep breath, missy, and start again. . . . Now, what's wrong?'

'It's G-Gabe,' she said between gulps of air. 'Th-they've got him!'

'Who has?'

'Some men – gunmen from across the border in Palomas.'

Emily gasped. 'Oh, dear God – when did this happen?'

'Last night! Gabe was in Columbus an' one of 'em recognized him—'

'Whoa,' Drifter said. 'I thought Gabe was hiding out in Mexico?'

'He was.'

'Then what was he doing in Columbus?' Emily asked.

'Ridin' up to see Momma. He don't usually cross the border there 'cause it's out of his way. But he saw a bunch of *rurales* near Cohiba, where he usually crosses, an' figured— Oh, it's all her fault,' Raven said tearfully. 'If only Momma had—'

'Never mind whose fault it is,' Drifter broke in. 'Just tell me who told you all this.'

'Gabe's friend – Agapita Barela.' Seeing the name didn't register with Drifter, Raven added, 'He's an ol' Mexican who used to work for us after Pa was killed. Gabe got Momma to hire him. Agapita was in this cantina in Columbus an' heard these gunmen braggin' 'bout how they were gonna spend the reward money – you know, the thousand dollars Mr Stadtlander's offerin' for Gabe's head.'

'Damn,' Drifter said softly. 'Where're they holding him, do you know?'

'Agapita wasn't sure. But he says the gunmen are holed up in the hills near the Tres Hermanas an' thinks that's most likely where they got Gabe.'

'What is the Three Sisters?' Emily asked.

'Three mountains off the Deming Road just west of Columbus,' Drifter explained. He turned back to Raven. 'Did Agapita mention where the gunmen intended to collect the reward?'

'What difference does that make?' Raven said.

'All the difference in the world: it would tell us if they're taking Gabe to Deming or Santa Rosa.'

'Oh.' Raven thought a moment. 'Now I remember. Momma asked him the same question an' Agapita said he wasn't sure.'

'Seems like there is a lot of things he is not sure about,' Emily said.

'What do you expect?' Raven said. 'He's just a poor ol' Mexican.'

'But he *is* sure that the man the gunmen are holding prisoner is Gabe?' Drifter pressed.

' 'Course he is. I know 'cause Momma asked him that too, an' he kept noddin' and twistin' his ol' hat in his hands, sayin', *"Estoy seguro, señora! Estoy seguro!"* '

'Well, if he's that positive,' Drifter said, 'we'll take him at his word and hope that we make the right choice. Because if we don't – if we ride to Deming and they take him to Santa Rosa – Stadtlander will get to Gabe before we can and that means . . . goodbye Gabriel Moonlight.'

'Do not say that,' Emily scolded. 'Don't even *think* that. We just have to make the right choice.'

'An' how do we do that?' Raven demanded.

Drifter ignored the question. 'Where's this fella Agapita now?' he asked her.

'At home with Momma.'

'Then that's where we're going.'

Raven, her boyishly short black hair reflecting the last rays of the setting sun, looked uneasy. 'Why? We'd just be farther away from both places.'

'But closer to the horse's mouth,' Drifter said. Seeing she didn't understand, he added, 'I want to talk to Agapita myself. See if I can get anything out of him that he might not have told you or your mother. Doesn't have to be much – just a word or two that one of the gunmen said that might tell us where they're taking Gabe.'

Raven grew even more uneasy. 'Well, you go where you want, mister. Me, I'm ridin' to Deming 'cause that's closer to Columbus an' it's where I think they'll take him.'

She started to walk away. Drifter grabbed her arm and forced her to face him. 'What's wrong? What's troubling you?'

'Nothin'—'

'Don't lie to me. Now tell me what's wrong!'

'N-Nothin's wrong. Now let me go!'

He stared hard into her big black eyes. 'Dammit, girl, you're lying. Something's bothering you. Now tell me what it is, or believe me, you won't be riding anywhere!'

Raven glared at him defiantly.

Emily, who'd been studying her intently, said, 'Let her go, Quint.'

Drifter frowned at her – saw something in her expression that made him trust her judgement and released Raven.

Emily fell in beside Raven, 'C'mon,' and accompanied her to her horse.

Drifter watched as the two girls reached the horse, paused, and began talking. He couldn't hear what they were saying. But their conversation was brief and animated. Then Raven grabbed the horse's mane and swung up on to its back. Emily motioned for her to wait and hurried back to Drifter.

'It's her mom. Raven took off without telling her.'

'Judas!'

'If I had been her I would have done the same thing.'

'Well, that makes me feel better,' Drifter said.

Ignoring his sarcasm, Emily said, 'She's worried that if she goes back home with us, her mom will not let her leave again.'

'I wouldn't blame her.'

'That is why I said you would help her.'

'Thanks. How?'

'Persuade her mother to either let Raven ride with us or for both of them to come with us when we go to Deming or Santa Rosa.'

'We?' Drifter said. 'What the hell makes you think I'd let you—'

'Oh, for God's sake,' Emily interrupted, 'don't start whipping that old horse again. 'Course I'm going with you. What is more,' she continued, before he could argue, 'if you cannot talk Mrs Bjorkman into agreeing, then Raven says she will run away again and go help Gabe by herself. And even *you* can surely see that that is more dangerous than if she rides along with us.'

Drifter stared at her, amazed by her gall. 'Judas,' he repeated. 'Great. Jumping. Judas.'

CHAPTER EIGHTEEN

Later, when Drifter explained to Ingrid about Gabriel Moonlight being captured by gunmen, she was just as insistent about going with them as Raven had been. When Drifter protested, she came and stood in front of him, looked at him with her blue, sincere eyes and said quietly, 'Mr Longley, I don't want you to think I'm feeling sorry for myself. I'm not. But the truth is, I am a widow in my thirties . . . a widow with a child . . . a girl, not even a boy who can help work the ranch. Marriage-wise that is the bottom of the barrel. So my choice of eligible husbands is limited to say the least. So when any man shows interest in me—'

'Goodgodalmighty,' Raven broke in. 'Why don't you tell him the truth?' Then as Ingrid glared at her, she said to Drifter, 'It ain't 'cause she's a widow or 'cause I'm a girl that she wants to go. Momma loves Gabe. Loves him an' misses him so much I hear her cryin' at night sometimes—'

'Raven, for pity's sake,' her mother began.

'It's the Bible-sworn truth,' Raven told Drifter. 'I

don't know what you're so mad about,' she said to Ingrid. 'I mean, hell's bells, I miss him so much I cry myself sometimes too.'

Her mother sighed, but offered no argument. 'Raven's right,' she admitted finally. 'I do love Gabe. And I do miss him more than I can stand sometimes.'

'No shame in that,' Drifter said, feeling her anguish.

'Then you understand why I insist on going with you? If anything happened to Gabe and I wasn't there I'd never forgive myself.'

Drifter shrugged. 'Well, I can't stop you from going, Mrs Bjorkman—'

'Please – Ingrid.'

'Ingrid, but I want to warn you, both of you,' he added, including Raven, 'either of you get in my way, or somehow tip off these gunmen why we're here, you could be jeopardizing Gabe's life. These scum smell blood money. And they'll stop at nothing to get it, including killing you or your daughter.'

'I understand,' Ingrid said quietly. 'No matter what the outcome, I will not hold you responsible for anything. Fair enough?'

'Fair enough,' Drifter said. He turned to the old Mexican, Agapita Berla, standing silently by the front door. A small, gentle-eyed man with shaggy white *pistolero* mustaches and a brown face that resembled wrinkled parchment, he spoke little English but seemed to understand everything that was going on. Drifter had only met him a few minutes ago but had taken an immediate liking to him.

'Go saddle their horses, *amigo.*'

'*Sí, señor.*' Agapita started out the door, paused and looked back at Drifter. '*Por favor, yo tambien querria ir con usted.*'

'Why the hell not?' Drifter said. 'Everyone else is getting into the act.'

Led by Agapita, who came from Palomas and was familiar with the territory on both sides of the border, the five of them rode all night and were only a mile or so from Columbus when dawn broke.

Already within sight of the Tres Hermanas Mountains, they camped behind a natural wall of boulders that offered them protection from the encroaching sun and rested until mid-morning. By then Agapita had built a fire and made coffee, something that further endeared him to Drifter. Cheerful and seemingly tireless, the old Mexican gave Drifter the names of two of the five gunmen he'd heard bragging about capturing Gabe in the cantina. Also, after much thinking, he described the other three.

'Forgive my ignorance,' he apologized. 'My ears should have listened better. Then perhaps I hear all their names.'

'You did fine, *amigo*,' Drifter assured him. 'If any of these weasels are still in Columbus, I'll find them.'

'Are you certain this is a good idea?' Emily asked, as her father saddled up and prepared to ride into town. 'If they get suspicious and decide to jump you, you could end up the same as Gabe. *Then* what will we do?'

'Come and rescue me of course.'

'I'm serious, Father.'

Drifter lost his grin. 'I'm going to be fine, just fine,' he assured her. 'You just be sure and stay hidden behind these rocks and do whatever Agapita says, all right?'

'You do not have to worry about me,' Emily said tartly. 'I am perfectly—'

'—capable of looking after yourself,' finished Drifter. 'Yes, I know. But for my sake, this one time do like I ask.'

'*As* I ask,' corrected Emily.

'That too,' Drifter said. He rolled his eyes at Ingrid, who seemed amused by the fact that someone other than herself had an irksome daughter. 'Same goes for you,' he added to Raven. 'Stay put, no matter what. Understand?'

As usual, she answered his question with a question. 'What if we hear shootin'? Or we see you bein' shot at by the gunmen?'

'No-matter-what,' repeated Drifter. 'Now, I want your word on it.'

Raven hesitated, loath to be pinned down.

'Go on,' Emily urged. 'Give him your word. It's for all our sakes.'

'Oh, all right,' Raven grumbled. 'I'll stay here. Promise.'

'Thanks. 'Preciate that.' Drifter tapped the sorrel's flanks with his spurs and rode off in the direction of Columbus.

CHAPTER NINETEEN

As usual strong winds were gusting in Columbus, filling the hot dry air with dust and sand. Wind-blown sand also muddied the sky and turned the sun a hazy orange color.

As Drifter rode between the scattering of adobe shacks and stores, he kept his neckerchief tied across the lower half of his face, enabling him to breathe without choking. Tumbleweeds went bouncing and spinning by. One of them bumped against the sorrel. The startled horse snorted and jumped sideways, almost unseating Drifter. But he quickly got the animal under control and rode on toward the rundown cantina. Several horses were tied up outside. Their saddles were old and worn, without any silver studs or conchos that Mexican ranchers favored, and Drifter guessed they belonged to local cowhands or the gunmen.

Dismounting, he took his time about looping the reins around the tie-rail, so that he could take in everything around him. A gaunt mongrel nosing for food in some garbage was the only sign of life on the street. Satisfied that no gunmen were posted as lookouts, Drifter went inside.

Inside, the men drinking along the bar were mostly local Mexicans. They stopped talking and looked to see who had just entered; then not recognizing Drifter, they returned to their conversations.

It was the same with the four cowboys drinking and playing poker at a table at the rear. After one glance at Drifter, they went back to their cards.

Disappointed that the gunmen holding Gabe were not here, Drifter ordered a beer from the surly, balding Mexican barkeep. Then, trying to appear furtive, he quietly asked him if he had seen any lawmen in town. When the man shook his head, Drifter placed a silver dollar on the bar and said: '*Usted seguro de eso?*'

'*Sí. Muy seguro.*'

Pretending that he was relieved, Drifter smiled and slid the dollar to the barkeep. Then putting another dollar on the bar he asked the man if he knew where Seth Engstead and Chris Toliver were. The barkeep shook his head and said he'd never heard of them. But his eyes flickered uneasily and Drifter guessed he was lying.

'That's too bad, *amigo.*' Drifter put a third dollar on the bar. 'I've heard they're holding an old enemy of mine, Mesquite Jennings, and plan to turn him in to the sheriff at Deming for the reward.'

Again, the barkeep looked uneasy.

'I'd give a month's wages to see that bastard dancing from a rope. 'Course,' Drifter added, retrieving the silver dollars, 'if you don't know Seth or Chris then I reckon I'm wasting my time.' Draining his beer, he started out.

'*Señor. . . .*'

Drifter turned and saw that the barkeep had moved down the bar to the end nearest the door. 'Yeah?'

'*Estos hombres, son amigos tuyos?*'

'Sure. We're close as brothers. And I know they were in here, *amigo*, 'cause my cousin heard them bragging about how they were gonna spend the reward money.'

The barkeep nervously ran his tongue over his straggly black mustache, then extended his chubby hand, palm up, to Drifter. 'For five dollar I tell you where they take this outlaw, Jennings.'

Drifter dug out three silver dollars and set them on the bar. 'That's all I got, *amigo*. Take it or leave it.'

The barkeep quickly pocketed the money, saying, 'Santa Rosa.'

'Not Deming?'

'No, *señor*. These *hombres*, and other men with them, they are not welcome in Deming.'

'*Cuando?*'

'*Hoy en algun momento.*'

'*Gracias.*' Drifter left. Outside the wind had died down and people now hurried along on the street. Drifter drank from his canteen, poured some water on his neckerchief and gently wiped the dust from around the sorrel's eyes. He then untied the reins, stepped up into the saddle and swung the horse around. It took a few amiable steps and then repaid Drifter's kindness by suddenly bucking.

But Drifter, ready for anything, wasn't thrown off. 'Ungrateful sonofabitch,' he said, slapping the sorrel with his hat. 'Latigo's right. I should put a goddamn round 'tween your eyes!'

'So what do we do now?' Emily asked, after Drifter had filled them all in with the news. 'I mean if they intend to take Gabe to Santa Rosa sometime today, as the bartender said, they could be miles ahead of us already.'

'I think we should assume they are,' Drifter said. 'That way, if we push our horses a little we should reach town not long after they do.'

'And if the bartender's mistaken and they haven't left yet,' Ingrid put in, 'what do we do then?'

Drifter shrugged. 'We got a choice. If we reach Santa Rosa ahead of them, I can ride back along the trail a piece and maybe get the drop on them – force them to hand Gabe over to me.'

'And if they are ahead of us and have already turned him over to Macahan?'

'Then I'll have to find a way to break him out of jail before Stadtlander hears of Gabe's capture and rides into town to hang him. Macahan will try to stop him,' he added, thinking aloud, 'but he'll be one man against thirty, maybe more. And not even Macahan can beat those odds.'

'Either way,' Raven said impatiently, 'we oughta quit talkin' an' get started.'

'For once,' her mother said, 'I agree with you.'

'*Señor, un momento, por favor. . . .*'

'What is it?' Drifter said, as Agapita stepped forward,

sombrero held humbly in his wrinkled hands.

'There is perhaps, I think, a faster way.'

'I'm listening.'

Agapita stood there a moment, eyes lowered, and then in poor, faltering English explained that he had relatives living just across the border. One of them, a nephew, was a cattle rancher who owned lots of horses. If asked, Agapita was sure he would loan them as many as they needed.

'But we already got horses,' Raven said impatiently. 'What do we want more for?'

'He's not talking about for you,' Drifter said, catching on. 'He means for me. Right, *amigo*?'

'*Sí, señor.*'

'I'll take two or three. That way I can ride each one till it's exhausted and then jump on Wilson and, hopefully, overtake the gunmen or at least reach Santa Rosa before them.'

'That's a great idea,' exclaimed Emily. 'We can pick the horses up on our way and return them later. *Muy bueno, señor,*' she told Agapita. '*Muy bueno!*'

'*Gracias, señorita.*'

'Well, let's get to it,' Drifter said, mounting up. 'Time's a-wasting.'

CHAPTER TWENTY

Riding hard, they crossed the border several miles east of Columbus and within thirty minutes reached the land owned by Agapita's favorite nephew, Noe Ruiz.

Unfenced, the *hacienda* covered fifty square miles of mostly sun-baked scrubland, but in the low hills and canyons not far from the actual ranch-house there was good grassland and a shallow creek, both fed by an underground river. Cattle and horses grazed content- edly on the grass, their only natural enemies being rattlesnakes and an occasional hungry mountain lion. Two adult sons, Clavo and Ciero, and a dozen hawkish, fierce-eyed *mestizos* protected the livestock and at the same time kept a sharp lookout for gringo rustlers.

Four of them now came riding across the desert toward Drifter and the others, their expressions growing less suspicious as they saw the men were accompanied by a woman and two young girls. The leader, a small wiry man wearing *vaquero* clothes and a black, silver-studded sombrero, blocked Drifter's path with his horse and gave a toothy smile.

'*Buenas tardes, señor,*' he said politely to Drifter. 'May I ask what you are doing here?'

Before Drifter could reply, Agapita spoke rapidly in Spanish to the man. Drifter didn't catch all of what he said, but he understood enough to know Agapita was reprimanding him, because the man immediately lost his smile and stiffened respectfully in the saddle. 'Forgive me, Don Barela. It has been many years. I did not recognize you.'

Agapito said sharply, 'We are in a hurry, *hombre.* Ride with us so we are not stopped again.' It was an order, not a request, and the man obeyed it without question. Barking orders to the other *mestizos,* he whirled his horse around and at a loping gait, led the way to the ranch-house seen a mile or so ahead.

Drifter, realizing that Agapita was more than the itinerant Mexican worker he pretended to be, grinned at the old Mexican, who slid him a sly wink.

As they neared the *casa del rancho* one of the *mestizos* galloped ahead to tell his patron that his Uncle Agapita was coming.

A few minutes later when Drifter and the others reined up in front of the house, Noe Ruiz was waiting for them on the porch. He was a handsome man. He had premature wavy silver hair, the same gentle brown eyes as his uncle, and a trimmed silver Van Dyke beard. Surprisingly tall for a Mexican, he looked lean and fit all in black and carried himself with great dignity. As Agapita dismounted, he hurried forward to greet him.

'*Bienvenido, bienvenido, mi tio! Es maravilloso verlo*

despues de todos estos anos!'

'It is good to see you too, my nephew,' Agapito replied, adding, 'I grow ashamed when I think how long my absence has kept us apart.'

'We will talk of this later,' Noe Ruiz said soothingly. 'But first, you and your *Norteamericano* friends must honor my house.' He stepped back, introduced himself and then invited Drifter, Ingrid and the girls to come inside.

Drifter lagged behind, saying, 'Señor Ruiz . . . I don't want to appear rude or offend you, but it's vitally important that I get to Santa Rosa as fast as I can.'

Before Ruiz could reply, Agapita quickly explained about Drifter's need for three horses.

'It is done,' Noe Ruiz said. He spoke rapidly to the *mestizos.* Vaulting into their saddles, they spurred their mounts toward a corral containing horses. 'It will not take long,' Ruiz told Drifter. 'While we wait, I insist that all of you accept my hospitality.'

'That is most kind of you, *señor,*' Ingrid said before Drifter could refuse. 'Come along, girls.' She led Emily and Raven into the large, single-story adobe house.

'First I'd like to water my horse,' Drifter said.

Ruiz nodded and called to a nearby vaquero, who came hurrying over. '*Esta caballo de agua!*' Ruiz told him. Then as the man led the sorrel to a water trough beside the barn, Noe Ruiz led Agapita, Drifter and the women indoors.

CHAPTER
TWENTY-ONE

Two *mestizos* escorted Drifter and the extra horses back
to the border. There they wished him well and watched
as he rode off in the direction of Santa Rosa.

The spirited, black maned bay he was riding bare-
back was built for stamina. The other two horses he was
leading – along with his sorrel, Wilson – were equally
leggy and deep-chested and Drifter was confident that
he would reach Santa Rosa ahead of the gunmen.

He had also caught a break with the weather: there
was little wind and the clouds overhead inched slowly
across the blue sky, for the most part keeping the broiling sun hidden. It was still hot, but nowhere near as hot
as it would have been had the sun been beating directly
down on him. Grateful, but knowing the cloud cover
probably would not last for the entire ride to Santa
Rosa, he pushed the horse harder than he'd antici-
pated doing. It responded gamely, and the miles and
flat scrubland sped past.

But at that pace the bay could only last so long and after an hour or so, it began to labor. Flecks of lather and foam from its gaping mouth flew back on to Drifter's shirt. He maintained the pace for another mile and then not wanting to kill the animal, dropped the reins and pulled the gray alongside him, drew his legs up under him and jumped on to its bare back.

Landing safely astride the galloping horse, he grasped the mane to steady himself then grabbed the reins and urged it onward.

The gray responded bravely. Off to his left the exhausted bay fell back and with heaving flanks, came to a stop. Drifter felt a moment of guilt for leaving the horse to the mercy of the desert. But he quickly assured himself that Agapita and the women would no doubt find it, and his mind returned to the business at hand.

As he rode, feeling the muscles of the loping horse rippling under his legs, he wondered if the gunmen had indeed started out before him and, if so, how many he would have to face once he overtook them and tried to rescue Gabe. Hopefully not more than two or three; then, with any luck, he could work his way around them and find some sort of cover so he could get the jump them. Of course, they wouldn't surrender Gabe easily – not with a thousand-dollar reward awaiting them. But right now that was the least of his worries. If there were more than three gunmen – say, six or eight of them – they would not give Gabe up but instead shoot it out with him. And the outcome of that uneven gunfight was not something Drifter wanted to think about; especially when he had a life with Emily to enjoy.

Of course there was always the chance that the gunmen weren't ahead of him. If that was the case he thought, then an even bigger challenge faced him: how to get Gabe out of jail under the watchful eye of Deputy US Marshal Macahan.

Before he could even consider how he would manage it, a rock pocket mouse darted in front of the gray, pursued by a low-swooping red-tailed hawk. It flew right in front of the horse, causing it to break stride and stumble.

Though caught off-guard, Drifter managed to let go of the rope holding the other horses and with both hands dragged back on the reins, trying to keep the gray's head up. It was impossible. The momentum of the horse couldn't be stopped and the gray went down on to its knees, pitching Drifter over its head.

He landed hard, felt himself rolling over and over, and slammed into a rock.

Momentarily everything was starry.

Then black.

When Drifter regained consciousness, a disgustingly ugly face stared down at him. It had an ivory-colored beak, purplish-red head and neck and glaring yellow eyes. Attached to the neck was a hunched-over black body.

Drifter blinked, hoping the image would disappear. But it was still there when he reopened his eyes and, worse, it now pecked at his cheek.

Still groggy, Drifter grunted from the painful bite; at the same time he instinctively swung his arm at the face, knocking it aside. The startled turkey buzzard screeched, angrily flapped its big wings and hopped off his chest. But as Drifter sat up and looked about him, he saw a half-dozen other vultures encircling him, eagerly awaiting his death.

Drifter yelled at them and waved his arms, causing the birds to hop back and then settle down again around him. Drifter started to get up but a wave of dizziness hit him, forcing him to sit back down. His head throbbed with pain. He gingerly felt his forehead, winced and saw blood on his lowered fingers.

Around him the boldest of the vultures now hopped closer.

Drifter reached for his six-gun. His hand grasped air and when he looked, he saw the holster was empty.

Another wave of dizziness hit him. Nauseated, he sank back and lay staring numbly at the sky. The wind had picked up, thinning out the clouds, allowing the sun to glare through. He felt it burning on his face. He then heard feathers rustling and talons scraping on the sand and knew the buzzards were closing in again. He wondered if he had enough strength to fight them off—

It was then he heard a shrill, angry scream followed by the sound of thudding hoofs. Forcing himself to rise up on one elbow, he saw the sorrel charging at the circle of buzzards, forcing them to burst aloft in fear. The enraged horse then wheeled around and reared up, forelegs pawing at the sky as if he was trying to hit the now-circling turkey buzzards.

Drifter heaved a sigh of relief. 'Thanks, Wilson,' he

said gratefully. Or did he imagine he said it and in fact just think it? He couldn't be sure. He couldn't be sure in fact about anything at that moment – except one thing. Of that he was very sure. He was damned glad he hadn't listened to Latigo and put a round between the cantankerous sorrel's eyes.

It took Drifter several minutes before his head cleared enough for him to consider getting up. By then the vultures were circling high overhead and the sorrel had calmed down and now stood patiently beside Drifter. Grabbing the dangling reins, Drifter pulled himself to his feet, waited for the world to stop spinning and then unhooked his canteen from the saddle horn. Unscrewing the cap he took a long swig. The water was warm and tasted like an old penny, but to Drifter, as he gulped it down, it was the sweetest tasting water in the world.

Next he untied his neckerchief, wetted it and gently pressed it over his face. The cool dampness against his scorched skin brought new life to him. Tying the wet neckerchief around his neck he then poured water into his cupped palm and held it under the sorrel's velvety mouth. The horse gulped it down. It then gently nipped Drifter's hand, but only with its soft lips, as if to remind him that it could have bitten him if it had wanted to. Drifter chuckled, despite himself, refilled his palm with water, waited for the sorrel to drink then recapped the canteen and hung it back on the horn.

'Wilson,' he said – and this time he was *sure* he said it, 'you are one hell of a horse!'

The leggy red sorrel tossed its head, its flaxen mane flashing in the sunlight, and snickered. Not trusting the horse, Drifter stepped back. But Wilson made no attempt to nip him; instead the sorrel swung its head around and looked at him, its amber-brown eyes filled with a kind of grudging, long-suffering tolerance.

'Don't give me that goddamn look,' Drifter growled. 'One good deed doesn't make up for all the other times you've tried to bite me, or kick the crap out of me.' Steadying himself, he looked around for his six-gun. It lay a dozen feet away, half-hidden by drifting sand. Drifter slowly led the horse over to the Colt, knelt and picked it up. Snapping the cylinder open, he blew the sand from it and from inside the barrel, and tucked the gun into his holster. Then, reins in hand, he stepped into the stirrup, grabbed the horn and pulled himself up on to the saddle. The effort made his head swim. Forcing himself to focus, he looked about him. The vast, flat, sun-baked scrubland was empty save for occasional clumps of mesquite, prickly pear and brownish patches of cat's claw – and beyond, in the distance, a range of steep mountains, their lower slopes green with ocotillo.

But no horses!

Drifter, realizing that he didn't have time to search for them, knew it was now up to the sorrel. Tapping the horse's flanks with his spurs, he rode off.

Knowing he had time to make up, he pushed the sorrel harder than he would have preferred. Despite the heat, Wilson responded without complaint. Grateful, Drifter made a promise with himself that when they reached town he would feed the horse the best oats he could find and let it enjoy a well-earned rest. Meanwhile, though, it was time to test the sorrel's vaunted stamina and ride like hell to Santa Rosa.

The miles fell behind them. So did the monotonous scenery. Flat sandy scrubland, scattered desert plants, occasional outcrops of rocks, a shallow gully here and there – a man could close his eyes, ride for hours and when he woke up he might think he hadn't moved. The suffocating heat combined with the rhythmic, rocking-chair loping gait of the sorrel made Drifter sleepy. Several times he almost dozed off. Wondering if his fall and still-throbbing head were part of the problem, he fought off sleep by keeping his mind busy . . . thinking of all the fun times he was going to enjoy with Emily; of how wrong he'd been not to tell her sooner that he was her father; and, worst of all, of how much love he had cheated them both out of by refusing to accept parental responsibility.

'Dammit,' he said aloud. 'Dammit all to hell!'

CHAPTER
TWENTY-TWO

Several hours behind him Agapita rode alongside
Ingrid, while Emily and Raven brought up the rear.
They rode at a steady, easy lope that ate up the miles
without exhausting the horses, and by late afternoon
came upon the bay. By now the horse had fully recov-
ered and was grazing contentedly on a patch of yellow
scrub-grass growing out of the bank of a shallow gully.

'*Espere aqui, por favor, señora,*' Agapita told Ingrid,
'*mientras que el caballo.*'

'No, I'll get him,' said Raven. Before they could stop
her, she wheeled her horse around and rode to the
gully.

Ingrid started to apologize to Agapita for her daugh-
ter's behavior, but he stopped her and smiled tolerantly.
'Do not scold her, *señora*. It is the way of the young.
Their feet take them where reason fears to tread.'

Emily laughed. 'I must remember that,' she told
Agapita. 'It will come in handy the next time my father

tells me not to do something.'

They rode on for another hour or so, all four riding abreast now with Raven leading the bay. It was too hot to talk; almost too hot to think. The only sound was made by their horses' hoofs, thud-thudding on the burning sand.

Presently, Raven gave a shout and pointed ahead. 'Look! There!' she called out. 'Ain't that the other two horses?'

Shading their eyes from the glaring sun, the others looked at where she was pointing and saw the gray and the ridgeback dun trotting toward them.

'Oh God,' Emily said, concerned. 'Something's happened to my father!'

'How do you know that?' Ingrid asked.

''Cause otherwise the horses wouldn't be together,' Raven said. 'They oughta be an hour or so apart. Like this one' – she indicated the bay – 'was.'

'*Su hija razon,* señora. *Esto es una mala senal, creo.*'

'See,' Raven said. 'Agapita agrees with me.'

'And I say we're all jumping to conclusions,' Ingrid insisted. 'There are plenty of reasons the horses are together . . . without it being a bad sign.'

'Name one,' Raven said.

'Well, for one thing,' her mother said, 'the second horse Quint used could have been looking for grass or something to eat, and was still here when the last horse decided to head back this way—'

'Or he could have been thrown,' Emily said quietly, not wanting to believe her own suggestion.

Agapita said to Ingrid, 'It is best, I think, if we. . . .'

111

He paused, trying to find the English words for what he wanted to say.

'Spread out?' she said, miming that they should ride farther apart.

'*Sí, señora.* But not so far we cannot see each other.'

'I agree,' Ingrid said. Then, to Emily, 'You take that side,' she pointed. 'Raven, you stay on the right. And both of you, I want to see you at all times. Understand?'

Emily and Raven nodded and rode off in opposite directions.

'And if either of you see any signs that indicate Mr Longley is hurt, blood or anything, stay on your horses and give a shout,' Ingrid called after them. 'You hear me, Raven? *Do not* get off your horse. Or next thing we know you'll get bitten by a rattler or Gila monster or something, and end up dying out here in the middle of nowhere!'

Without turning, the girls waved to show they heard Ingrid and continued riding.

It was silent then except for the faint moaning of the wind – a wind that carried Raven's words back to Ingrid and Agapita.

'Goodgodalmighty,' she grumbled. 'To hear Momma talk, a person'd think we didn't have a brain in our heads.'

CHAPTER
TWENTY-THREE

Canyon del Lobo did not get its name because it once was inhabited by wolves, but because of a large sandstone rock at the west entrance that eons of wind had carved into the shape of a wolf's head.

As Drifter rode past the rock, he felt a sense of relief knowing that he was now only three miles from Santa Rosa. Under him the sweat-soaked sorrel was beginning to labor but still performing magnificently. 'Hang in there, Wilson,' he encouraged the harsh-breathing horse. 'Few more miles and—' He broke off as the sorrel faltered, took a few more hesitant strides then pulled up lame.

'Shit!' Drifter quickly slid from the saddle and stood there, reins in hand, watching as the lathered horse limped around him, favoring its right foreleg.

'Whoaaa. . . . Easy, boy, easy,' Drifter said soothingly. Moving close, he lifted the injured leg and checked the hoof. The horseshoe was missing and blood seeped from a deep stone bruise. Swearing under his breath, Drifter gently lowered the hoof to the ground and unhooked his canteen from the saddle. 'Reckon we're done for the day, Wilson.' Unscrewing the cap, he poured water into his cupped palm and let the horse drink from it. He then took a swig himself before replacing the cap. He looked about him, wondering if the gunmen holding Gabe had already passed through here or if they were behind him. On impulse, he took his field-glasses from his saddle-bag and led the sorrel across the narrow canyon to the foot of the south wall. The cliffs on both sides were not particularly high, or steep, but he knew if he climbed to the top he'd have a clear view all the way to town. If the gunmen *were* ahead of him but hadn't yet reached Santa Rosa, he would be able to see them – then he'd at least know the kind of hand he'd been dealt. Draping the glasses around his neck, he began scrambling up between the rocks.

Ten minutes later, he reached the top. Winded and soaked in sweat, he sat on a rock and scanned the open flatlands stretching from the canyon to Santa Rosa. Focusing the lenses, he swept the area. At first he saw no sign of life. Then, sure enough, less than a mile from the outskirts a group of riders popped into view.

Propping his elbows on his knees, he steadied the glasses and got his first look at the gunmen. There were seven of them. All heavily armed, four rode ahead of Gabriel Moonlight; three behind him. Drifter focused on Gabe. The tall, wide-shouldered outlaw seemed unhurt – though Drifter could only see his friend from behind – but his hands were roped to the saddle horn

114

and he was missing his six-gun and rifle. Drifter lowered the glasses and grunted. Even if he had caught up with the gunmen, he realized, this kind of lawless border trash never would have surrendered Gabe to him – not without gunplay.

OK, he thought grimly. Now all he had to do was to come up with a plan to break Gabe out of jail – and soon! Because once word reached Stillman J. Stadtlander that his hated nemesis was behind bars, the rancher would bring all his men into town with only one thought in mind: a lynching!

It was late afternoon when a dusty, weary Drifter led his badly limping sorrel into Gustafson's Livery. At first the spotlessly clean stable appeared empty. But then Drifter heard someone curse in back, and moving forward saw Lars sitting on an upturned crate in near one of the stalls, sucking his thumb. He muttered something unintelligible as he saw Drifter approaching and then taking his thumb from his mouth, said: 'Yesus, you'd think after all these years I'd be able to sew somethin' without puttin' a goddamn hole in my thumb, wouldn't you?'

Drifter, now close enough to see that the small, gray-bearded Swede was repairing the hobble strap of a roping stirrup, said, 'Serve you right, you ol' bastard, for not wearing your spectacles.'

'Wear 'em?' snorted Lars. 'How can I wear the damn things if'n I can't see well enough to find 'em?'

Drifter leaned forward and with his forefinger pushed the spectacles resting atop Lars' forehead down on to his nose. 'That help?' he said.

'Well, by the bear that bit me.' Lars grinned sheep-ishly. 'Gettin' old's hell, ain't it?' Then noticing the dried blood on Drifter's forehead, he asked, 'What happened to you?'

'It's a long story. And right now I'd sooner you worried about Wilson than me.'

'Why, what's ailin' him?' On seeing how the sorrel was favoring its right foreleg, he added, 'Stone bruise?'

'It's worse'n that. Looks like he's cut right through to the coffin bone.'

Lars made a face and setting the stirrup aside, rose and hobbled over to the sorrel. 'Hold his head,' he told Drifter. 'Don't want the ornery sonofabitch bitin' me while I got my back turned.'

Drifter grabbed the bridle and kept the horse's head facing front while Lars examined the injured hoof. It didn't take long. 'Yesus,' he muttered, wincing with pain as he straightened up. 'That be one ugly cut.'

'Can you fix it?'

'A vet could fix it better.'

'Nearest vet's in Las Cruces.'

'That there do present a problem,' admitted Lars. 'Though I heared he's got a son thinkin' 'bout openin' an office here soon.'

Drifter said, 'It's mainly just a matter of keeping him off that foot, isn't it?'

'That'n keepin' the wound clean. But I got salves for that. Yah, reckon I can fix him. But it'll take a spell, so you'll need another horse.'

'Got one?'

'Matter of fact I do. Foller me.' Lars led Drifter to a

116

rear stall and pointed at the horse roped off inside. 'Reckon you know this ugly fella, huh?'

'Guess I do,' Drifter said wryly. He looked at the magnificent all-black Morgan stallion that belonged to Gabriel Moonlight and shook his head, adding: 'Mind if I ask you something?'

'Fire away.'

'Any of those weasels who turned Gabe in lay claim to Brandy?'

'Fella who did all the talkin' tried, but Deputy Macahan told him to shut his face. Said everyone knew the stallion belonged to Mr Stadtlander, and that put a lock on it.'

'So there's no doubt that by now Stadtlander knows Gabe's in jail?'

Lars snorted disgustedly. 'What d'you think?' He hobbled off, rubbing his arthritic lower back and began rummaging through a box of salves.

'Give Wilson the best of everything,' Drifter told the old Swede.

'When don't I?' Lars snorted, offended.

But Drifter had already walked out and was heading for the water trough to wash the blood from his forehead.

The door of the sheriff's office was propped by a rusty anvil, but inside it was still over-hot. Deputy US Macahan sat behind his desk, flyswatter in his upraised hand, intently following the flight of a horse-fly buzzing around his head.

'You got five minutes,' he said, as Drifter entered.

Then, eyes never leaving the fly, he held out his free hand, adding, 'But I'll need your gun.' As he finished talking the fly settled on the rim of a mug on the desk and the lawman smashed it with the swatter. The blow killed the fly but it also knocked over the mug, coffee dregs spilling over two nearby Wanted posters.

'Reckon you won't be pinning those on your wall,' Drifter said drily.

'No need to,' Macahan replied, spreading his kerchief over the puddle of spilled coffee. 'These two plug-heads are already dead. Now how about that gun?'

Drifter drew his .45, spun it on his finger and handed it butt-first to the tall, lean lawman. Macahan dropped it into the bottom drawer, removed a ring of keys and locked the drawer then led Drifter to the iron- barred-door leading back to the cells. Unlocking it, he stepped back so Drifter could enter, 'Remember – five minutes,' then relocked the door and returned to his desk to clean up the mess.

CHAPTER TWENTY-FOUR

Gabriel Moonlight lay stretched out on a bunk in the end cell. By the sunlight streaming in through the barred window, Drifter could see that he had his arms folded behind his head and through half-closed eyes was watching the smoke drifting upward from the cigarette slanted from his mouth. Except for a few cuts and bruises caused by knuckles beating on his face, he seemed as relaxed and contented as a man whiling away an afternoon in a hammock.

Drifter looked at him through the bars. 'I hate to disturb your siesta, *amigo*, but there's an old friend of yours riding this way with about thirty of his guns to invite you to a party.'

Gabe chuckled. 'A *necktie* party, yeah, I been expectin' him.' Swinging his legs over the side of the bunk, he sat up, yawned, stretched, and gingerly felt his swollen face. 'Lately, seems like folks got nothin' but my good health on their mind.' Pausing, he ran his fingers through his unruly black hair, then deadpanned, 'An' me, such a handsome an' obligin' fella, too.'

'Damn fool's more like it!' said Drifter. 'Judas, Gabe, what the hell were you thinking, being anywhere near Palomas or Columbus after all the trouble we caused last time we were there? I mean, do you *wanna* get hanged?'

Gabe grunted. 'You here to lecture or help me?' he demanded.

'Not sure you deserve either,' Drifter said. 'I know you don't give two smokes for most things, or most people, but do you have even the remotest idea of how much goddamn trouble you've caused?'

'I'm sure you're gonna tell me,' Gabe said. Rising, he sauntered up to the bars and fixed his unusually light-blue eyes on Drifter. 'Got the makin's on you?'

Drifter dug out a tobacco pouch and papers from his shirt, and passed them through the bars.

' 'Bliged.'

'If you got any ideas on how I can get you out of here, now would be the time to share them.'

Gabe tipped tobacco on to the paper, rolled the paper carefully between his fingers, licked the edge, sealed it and stuck the cigarette between his lips. Then pressing his face against the bars he looked expectantly at his friend.

Drifter sighed, dug out a match, flared it and lit Gabe's smoke.

'Nary a one,' Gabe said, spitting out a stream of smoke. 'You?'

He appeared so unconcerned Drifter wanted to hit

him. Instead, he said grimly, 'Right now, I don't even have a goddamn horse.' Turning, he marched to the door and yelled, 'Macahan! Open up!'

'I'll be here,' Gabe said laconically. He returned to his bunk, stretched out, blew a smoke ring and watched it drift lazily toward the ceiling.

In the sheriff's office Macahan unlocked the bottom drawer of his desk and took out Drifter's Colt. 'Want some advice?' he said grimly.

'Is it free?'

'Depends on what you do with it.'

'Gotta hear it before I can answer that.'

The deputy marshal handed the black-grip .45 to Drifter and nodded in the direction of the cells. 'Quit wastin' your time on him. He ain't worth it.'

'You don't know him well enough to say that.'

'I know he's trouble. A fast gun who never met a law he couldn't break.'

Drifter shrugged. 'Gabe's trouble, I'll admit. But not because he's mean through. He just believes in living life the way the rest of us would if we didn't have a conscience.'

'Or integrity.'

'Being a man means being responsible, that it?'

'No one's ever said it better.'

Drifter pinned the young deputy marshal with a hard look. Macahan met his gaze and held it steadfastly. Neither man spoke for several seconds.

'Hope you still feel that way,' Drifter said, 'when Stadtlander and his men ride in.'

'There'll be no lynchin', if that's what you're worried about.'

121

'One gun against thirty – just how you plan on preventing it?'

'I'll play that hand when it's dealt.'

Drifter smiled mirthlessly and moved to the window. He looked out at the near-empty sun-drenched street. 'Heat's keeping folks indoors.'

'Been like that all week.' Macahan fanned himself with one of the soggy wanted posters. 'But just like bats, they'll be out after sundown.'

'Just in time to watch Stadtlander and his boys ride in.'

'I reckon.'

Drifter turned back to Macahan. At the same time he drew his Colt from its holster and spun it on his finger.

The young deputy stiffened but didn't go for his gun.

'You know, Ezra, nobody'd blame you if you got a powerful thirst and had sudden urge to quench it in the cantina 'cross the street.'

'Don't 'spect they would.'

'And if your prisoner managed to break out while you were gone, they couldn't blame you for that, either.'

'Seems reasonable.'

'You think that might happen?' Drifter asked.

'Not while I got a breath in my body.'

Drifter expelled his frustration in a long sigh. 'Didn't think so.' He extended his free hand, palm up, adding, 'I'll take my shells now.'

Macahan looked mildly surprised. Then he dug out a handful of .45 shells from his pocket and handed them to Drifter.

Drifter pocketed them and then holstered his gun. 'See you around,' he said and started out.

'Quint. . . .'

Drifter turned and looked at the young lawman.

'How'd you know?'

Drifter grinned. 'It's what I would've done,' and walked out.

CHAPTER
TWENTY-FIVE

It was just before sundown when Emily, Ingrid, Raven and Agapita – now leading the three extra horses belonging to his nephew – rode into Santa Rosa.

Drifter, seated on the water trough outside the livery stable, saw them before they saw him and rose to greet them. They all looked as exhausted as their horses.

Emily smiled, relieved, when she saw Drifter. Quickly dismounting, she hurried to his side. 'W-What happened?' she asked. 'When we saw the gray and the dun together—'

'I'll explain later,' her father said. 'How about you – you all OK?'

'Yes, yes, we're fine,' Ingrid said. 'What about Gabe – and the gunmen?'

'I haven't run into the gunmen,' Drifter said. 'But most likely they're whooping it up at the Copper Palace. As for Gabe, he's grabbing forty in jail.'

'Forty?'

'Winks.'

'Ahh. . . .' Agapita said, smiling. '*El tiene mucho coraje, me parece.*'

'Courage, huh?' Drifter said drily. 'And here, all along I've been thinking he just didn't give a hoot.'

'A little of both is probably right,' Ingrid said.

'Go ahead,' Raven broke in angrily. 'Poke fun at him. Gabe's worth all of you put together. What's more,' she added, 'while you're all standin' around takin' shots at him, I'm goin' to the sheriff's office an' see how he is.'

'You'll do no such thing,' said her mother, grabbing her arm. 'You'll stay here and do what you're told.' Then turning to Drifter she asked, 'Seriously, is he all right?'

'Sure. The gunmen gave him a few lumps, but else-wise he's fine.'

'*Perdone, señor – que pasa con el Sr Stadtlander?*'

Drifter shrugged at the old silver-haired Mexican. 'My guess is he and his men are already riding this way.'

Emily said, 'Then we must hurry and get Gabe out of there.'

'Deputy Macahan might have something to say about that.'

'Well, we can't just stand around talkin',' Raven said.

'Be quiet,' Ingrid told her.

Raven ignored her. 'There's only one of him,' she said to Drifter, 'an' five of us. He can't shoot us all at once. An' if you keep him busy I bet I can sneak in there an' find the keys – let Gabe out.'

'I'm warning you—' her mother began.

'No, wait a minute,' said Drifter. 'Maybe Raven's got

125

a point.' They all turned to him. 'Agapita, you and I will ride around in back of the jail. We'll take an extra horse for Gabe and when we reach the window—'

'What do you want us to do?' Emily interrupted.

'I'm coming to that. You three go into the office and try to persuade Deputy Macahan into letting Gabe go before Stadtlander and his crew get here. He'll never agree, of course, but you keep on begging. Make as much fuss as you can. A little crying wouldn't hurt. Even a hard-nose like Macahan should have a soft spot for tears, especially coming from two young girls.'

'What're you going to be doing all this time?' Ingrid asked.

'Aw, Momma,' Raven chimed in, 'can't you figure nothin' out? Him an' Agapita are gonna tie ropes around the bars an' pull out the window so Gabe can escape.'

'Is that right?' Ingrid asked Drifter. 'Is that really what you intend to do?'

'Unless you got a better plan.'

'But that will make both of you outlaws, too.'

'Everything has its price,' Drifter said. Then to Agapita, 'That OK with you, *amigo*?'

'*Sí, señor.* It is time, I think, that I return to my own country anyway.'

'Then the rest is up to you three,' Drifter said to the women.

'Don't worry,' Emily said. 'We won't let you down, Father.'

'Never thought you would. Oh, one other thing: if Agapita and I are lucky enough to break Gabe out and get away, everyone's going to say you were part of it. But so long as you stick together, keep denying you were involved, no one can prove you're lying. Can I count on you to do that?' he said, addressing them all.

'Absolutely,' Ingrid said. 'Don't worry about us. You just take care of yourselves. You're the ones the law is going to come after.'

'*And* Mr Stadtlander,' Emily reminded. 'Don't forget about him. Or me,' she said directly to Drifter. 'Because once you do this, Father, he will never forgive you – just as he has never forgiven Gabe. He will keep sending men after you – bounty hunters like Latigo Rawlins – for as long as he lives . . . or until he catches you and hangs you. Which means,' she added darkly, 'you won't be able to come and see me at school in Las Cruces.'

'Don't think I haven't thought about that,' Drifter said grimly. 'But the idea of Gabe getting strung up for something he never did. . . .' He left the rest unsaid.

'It's all right, I understand,' Emily said. For the first time tears welled in her lovely brown eyes. 'In fact I could not live with myself if I thought I was the reason you didn't at least try to help him.'

Drifter nodded, knowing she meant it. But that didn't make it any easier.

No one seemed to know what to say next.

There was a long silence save for the sounds of horse-traffic passing along Main Street.

'*Por favor, señor,*' began Agapita.

'I know, I know,' Drifter said. 'We have to get going.' He put his arms lovingly around his daughter and hugged her as if it was the last time he'd ever get to do it.

CHAPTER TWENTY-SIX

Once the sun dipped below the distant sierras Santa Rosa came alive.

Though the temperature still hovered around one hundred degrees, the townspeople emerged from their homes and businesses and soon the cantinas, stores, streets and sidewalks bustled with activity.

Recently installed street lights glowed yellowy in the dusk. But few if any people noticed Ingrid, Emily and Raven as they crossed Main Street and headed for the sheriff's office.

'Now remember,' Ingrid told the girls, 'don't say any-thing until I ask Deputy Macahan to let Gabe go.'

'Momma, you already told us that more'n a hundred times!'

Ingrid ignored her daughter and continued to Emily, 'Because, as your father said, it's important the deputy and everyone else believes that that's the only reason we're there. But once he turns me down, then both of you chime in at once – turn on the waterworks

128

if you have to, but keep begging and begging for him to change his mind.'

They had reached the boardwalk fronting the office. Ingrid paused to let some pedestrians pass, then took a deep breath and stuck out her jaw determinedly. 'Ready?' she asked the girls.

They nodded, equally determined.

'Then in we go.'

At that same moment Drifter and Agapita, leading a spare horse, rode into the alley that divided the rear of the sheriff's office-and-jail from a row of adobe buildings. The alley was empty and dark. The only light came from the windows of the two-story Azteca House, which directly overlooked the jail.

Voices and raucous laughter could be heard inside the popular boarding-house and somewhere a piano played. Drifter and Agapita reined up across from the rear entrance, and made sure that no one was looking out of any of the brightly-lit windows.

Drifter then rode up close to the three small, barred windows of the jail. Standing up in the stirrups, he peered between the bars of the end window and could dimly make out Gabriel Moonlight lying on his bunk.

'Gabe!' he hissed.

Gabriel sat up, saw Drifter's face pressed against the bars and, jumping up, hurried to the window.

'What the hell—?' he began.

'Shut up and stand back!' Drifter said. Then, as Gabe obeyed, Drifter tied one end of his rope around two of the four bars embedded in the adobe and quickly backed up his horse.

Agapita then rode close to the window, tied his rope to the other two bars and backed his horse up alongside Drifter. Then each wrapped the other end of his rope around his saddle horn and urged his horse forward until the rope grew taut.

Drifter raised one hand as a signal. '*Listo?*'

'*Sí, señor.*'

Drifter, about to drop his hand, stopped as the rear door of the boarding-house swung open and light flooded the alley.

'Hold it!'

Drifter and Agapita turned and saw a short, slim, handsome man with curly blond hair standing in the doorway. The light reflected off the double-barreled shotgun he was aiming at them.

'For Chris'sake!' Drifter said. 'What the hell're you doing here?'

'Savin' you from goin' to jail,' Latigo Rawlins said. 'Now, drop those ropes, *amigo. Pronto!*'

Drifter didn't move. 'You know who's in that jail?'

'Sure.'

'We don't break him out, Lefty, Stadtlander will hang him. You want that?'

Latigo's amber-colored eyes hardened. 'What I want don't amount to a bag of peanuts. You take a man's wages, you do what he says.'

'Stadtlander!' Drifter said, disgusted. 'I should've known.'

'*Usted dejaria que su amigo pasar por unos cuanto dolares?*'

'Shut your face, Mex,' Latigo snarled at Agapita. 'Your life's hangin' from a thread as it is.' Turning back to Drifter, he added, 'Yeah, this is about money. So what? Gabe's full-growed. He knowed what he was riskin' by crossin' the border, an' now he's got to pay for it.' He thumbed back both hammers. 'Now, for the last time – drop them ropes.'

Drifter had seen that cold-eyed look many times before. He had seen what followed it, too – death. 'Do as he says,' he told Agapita. Then as the old *pistolero* obeyed, he dropped his own rope, said, 'What happens now? We all wait for your boss to arrive and then watch while Gabe's lynched?'

Latigo shrugged. 'That ain't my call.'

'But it *is* what'll happen – you know that as sure as I do.'

'What I know,' Latigo said flatly, 'is I didn't have to give you a chance. I could've gunned you down, both of you, an' gotten a medal for it.'

'Come to think it, Lefty, why didn't you shoot us?'

'Keep proddin' me, an' I still might,' the dapper little gunfighter said. 'Now git, 'fore I change my mind.'

Drifter nodded at Agapita, who grabbed the rope of the spare horse, and the two of them rode out of the alley.

A few minutes later they reined up in front of the sheriff's office. Signaling for Agapita to stay on his horse, Drifter dismounted, looped his reins over the hitch-rail and went inside.

He found Ingrid and the girls seated in front of

Deputy US Marshal Macahan, who sat calmly at his desk, unmoved by their impassioned pleading. He looked relieved – and surprised – to see Drifter, and, rising, said, 'You're just in time to escort your daughter and the Bjorkmans out of here.' He gave them a withering look. 'Few more minutes and they might've out-stayed their welcome.'

'What're you doing here?' Drifter said, as if surprised to see the women. 'You're supposed to be at the livery stable. Agapita and I have been looking all over for you.'

Emily, Ingrid and Raven, whose surprise at seeing him was real, now got to their feet and crowded around him.

'He won't let Gabe out,' Raven cried.

'We told him about Mr Stadtlander and his men, but he doesn't care,' Emily said through faked tears. 'I hate him!'

'Hush, dear,' Ingrid said. Then to Drifter, 'We were trying to persuade Deputy Macahan to let Gabe out of jail before he gets lynched—'

'There ain't gonna be a lynchin',' Macahan said firmly. 'Why won't you believe me?' Before they could reply, he added to Drifter, 'Frankly, I'm surprised to see you.'

'What're you talking about?'

'Well, I figured maybe you'd put them up to it.'

'Me? Are you loco?' Drifter said. 'Hell, I'd never ask a woman to belly up to the bar for me – and that goes double for young'uns. Come on, ladies,' he said, herding the three of them toward the door. 'Emily's got to get up early tomorrow. She's catching the morning train for Las Cruces.'

Outside, they paused on the boardwalk, where Drifter quickly explained what had happened in the alley. Emily, in particular, was shocked by what she felt was Latigo Rawlins's betrayal.

'I'll never talk to him again,' she said angrily. 'How could he? You and Gabe are his friends.'

'Mr Rawlins has no friends,' Ingrid said, looking at Drifter. 'Isn't that right?'

He nodded, 'Especially when it comes to money.' He looked off up the street as if expecting to see Stadtlander and his men at any moment. Then turning to Agapita, who was still on his horse, he said: 'Take Mrs Bjorkman and the girls back to the stable, will you?'

'*Sí, señor.*'

'What about you?' Emily asked. 'Aren't you coming too?'

'I'll be along in a few minutes,' Drifter assured them. 'Soon as I'm through talking to Macahan.'

'But—'

'Do as I ask,' Drifter said, gently pushing her aside.

'Yes, come along, girls,' Ingrid said, herding them on along the boardwalk. As she followed them, she glanced behind her and locked gazes with Drifter. Eyes full of trust, she smiled to assure him that she would look after Emily for him, and then facing front was swallowed up by the people crowding by.

Drifter took another long hard look up the street in the direction he guessed Stadtlander and his men would be coming. There was still no sign of them. Expelling his frustration in a weary sigh, he entered the sheriff's office.

CHAPTER
TWENTY-SEVEN

'You again?' Macahan said drily as Drifter plopped into a chair across the desk from him. 'Don't tell me that you've come to plead that saddle-tramp's case?'

'Not me,' said Drifter, rolling a smoke. 'I already tried that and I never make the same mistake twice.'

'Glad to hear it.' Macahan bit off a chew and tongued the tobacco into his cheek. 'I'm gettin' powerful weary of tellin' folks no. But I am curious to know why you're here,' he added, leaning back and putting his feet up.

'Maybe I just like being around a famous lawman.'

'In a burro's ass,' Macahan said affably. He pinned Drifter with a steely-eyed look. 'Wouldn't be because you think I'll need your help when Stadtlander and his boys bust in here, would it?'

'You've had worse ideas, Ezra.'

'Think they're gonna buffalo me, that it?'

'Don't you?'

Macahan slid his boots off the desk and leaned forward, so that the front legs of his chair slammed on to the floor. 'Goddammit,' he exploded. 'When're you people gonna start havin' a little faith in me?'

Knowing he hadn't finished, Drifter kept quiet.

'No one gave me this badge out of pity, or 'cause I was some fancy-pants senator's son – I earned the sonofabitch with spilled blood!'

'Never heard different,' Drifter said quietly. 'Never heard your name mentioned with anything but respect, either. It's just. . . .'

'Just what?'

'You haven't had many dealings with Stillman J. Stadtlander. If you had, and I don't mean this disrespectfully, you wouldn't be wondering why everyone figures you're in over your head.'

'That include you?'

'No. But I do think you're underestimating the man. He's ruthless and mean as a trod-on snake besides. Got a black hole where his heart should be. Worse, he ain't all bluster and posturing, either. He's killed more than one man who's gotten in his way and run roughshod over a hundred others.'

'Yeah, but how many of 'em were from the US marshal's office?'

'None. But that's only 'cause he sidesteps the law any time it tries to rope him, and when they holler foul he calls in his markers from Washington.'

Macahan prodded his chew into the opposite cheek and spat into the coffee can on the floor beside the desk. 'Wouldn't be tryin' to rattle me, would you?'

Drifter laughed mirthlessly. '*No one* rattles you, Ezra. So don't play humble pie with me. It doesn't suit you.'

Macahan thought a moment before saying, 'Tell you what: if I can't do the job I was sworn in to do, you'll be the first *hombre* I'll deputize to help me. Fair enough?'

'Fair enough,' Drifter said. He ground his smoke out under his heel and got to his feet.

Macahan waited until Drifter reached the door, then said, 'It's what I would've done, Quint.'

Then as Drifter turned and frowned at him, 'Had the widow and the girls keep pesterin' me while you'n the Mex tried to break Gabe out through the window.'

Drifter said, 'I don't know what the hell you're talking about, Macahan.' But he was chuckling as he walked out.

CHAPTER
TWENTY-EIGHT

When Drifter returned to the livery stable he was immediately surrounded by Emily, Ingrid and Raven, all clamoring to know if he had managed to persuade Macahan to release Gabriel before Stadtlander rode in.

'Simmer down,' Drifter told them. 'I can't understand you if you all talk at once.' Then as they grudgingly subsided, 'Macahan and I didn't discuss Gabe. That wasn't why I wanted to talk to him.'

'It wasn't?' Emily said, surprised.

'Uh-uh.'

'What, then?'

Drifter looked long and hard at his daughter. 'Before I go to war with a man, Emily, I like to test his mettle. See if he's got sand enough to stare down death.'

'And Macahan,' Ingrid asked, 'does he?'

Drifter shrugged his wide shoulders. 'Only way we'll

know for sure is when the time comes. But my gut tells me yes – right to his last spit.'

Raven said, 'Won't matter anyways. If it's only him against thirty, like you said, what chance has he got?'

Before anyone could reply, there was the sound of riders approaching.

'Reckon we'll soon find out,' Drifter said grimly.

As they hurried to the doorway, they were joined by Agapita and Lars Gustafson, who'd been playing checkers. They all looked out.

The sight they saw was chilling.

Crossing the railroad tracks and riding into town was Stadtlander and forty of his hands. Each man packed a Winchester and at least one six-shooter, some with two, others with a belly gun tucked into their jeans. All were grim-faced and eager to fight; especially Stadtlander's son, Slade, and the Iverson brothers, Mace and Cody.

But that wasn't what infuriated Emily. 'Look,' she exclaimed, pointing at Stadtlander's horse, 'he's riding Diablo!'

Stadtlander was indeed riding Emily's stallion. A blue roan with light blue eyes, the horse stood sixteen hands at the shoulder and was blessed with a smooth, effortless stride. Its proudly held head, long flowing mane and tail were black as Raven's hair, while its body appeared to be a silvery-blue color flecked in places with tiny white markings.

It was Drifter's first sight of the stallion and other than Gabe's all-black Morgan, Brandy, he had never seen a more magnificent horse.

139

'Isn't he beautiful?' breathed Emily.

'He is indeed,' her father agreed. 'Now I know why you were willing to risk everything to get him back.'

'And I will,' she said determinedly. 'No matter how much that hateful old man tries to stop me.' She glared at Stadtlander as he rode past the stable with his heavily-armed men, but the ruthless, jut-jawed rancher never looked her way.

'Look, Momma!' Now it was Raven's turn to point. 'There's that gunfighter, Latigo whatever his last name is.'

They looked and saw she was right: bringing up the rear, some five horse-lengths behind the dust kicked up by the riders, was Latigo Rawlins. Recently shaved, he wore a tan Stetson, fringed buckskin shirt, and rode a liver-colored Appaloosa that looked as if its rump was blanketed with snow.

'W-what's he doing with Mr Stadtlander?' said Emily, surprised.

'Earning wages,' Drifter said.

Emily grasped his arm, said urgently, 'Father, you can't outdraw him.'

'I know that,' Drifter said.

Something in his fierce gray eyes told her that he still intended to throw in with Macahan.

'He'll kill you. You know that, don't you?'

'What would you have me do – run and hide?' Before she could answer, he kissed her on the forehead and went to his saddle that hung over the stall containing his sorrel, pulled the Winchester out of its scabbard and returned beside them.

'*Espere, señor. Yo voy a ir con usted,*' Agapita said.

'Be proud to have you,' Drifter said.

Lars, noticing that the Mexican only had an old single-action pistol tucked into his pants, grabbed a shotgun leaning against a stall and tossed it to him. 'Here. This might come in handy.'

Agapita caught the shotgun, '*Mucho gracias, mi amigo,*' broke it open to show it was loaded, then snapped it shut and moved alongside Drifter.

' 'Fore either of you say anything,' Drifter told Emily and Raven, 'you're not coming.'

'I don't have to listen to you,' Raven said angrily. 'You ain't my pa.'

'But I'm your mother and you *do* have to listen to me,' Ingrid told her. 'And believe me, you're not going.'

'But Gabe's my friend—'

'He's my friend, too,' put in Emily.

'Then act like it,' Drifter said, speaking to both girls. 'If you two are around when the shooting starts – should it come to that – Agapita and I would be so worried about you, we wouldn't be any use to Deputy Macahan *or* Gabe.'

'Señor Longley, he is right,' Agapita said gently to Raven. 'This time it is better you listen than argue.'

Raven made a face. 'Grownups!' she said disgustedly. 'Can always find ways to make sense out of tellin' us not to do somethin'.'

'You want to do something,' Drifter replied, 'then help Mr Gustafson saddle up all our horses. If things don't go as planned, we'll need to get out of here in

one hell of a hurry.' With a nod to Ingrid, he led
Agapita out of the stable and on down Main Street
toward the sheriff's office.

CHAPTER TWENTY-NINE

Stillman J. Stadtlander was many things – most of them unpleasant – but one thing he wasn't was a coward.

Watched by almost everyone in town, he led his men along Main Street and stopped only when he was right in front of the sheriff's office. Behind him the Double S riders did the same. There were so many of them, they filled the street. Stadtlander signaled to them to line up on either side of him. Waiting until they were in position, he then barked, 'Remember what I told you, boys: nobody touches their gun till I give the order!'

Facing front, he rested both hands on the saddle horn and looked at the tall, broad-shouldered, lean-hipped man who had just stepped out of the office.

' 'Evenin', Macahan.'

'Deputy US Marshal Macahan – Mr Stadtlander.'

The short, burly, ageing rancher gritted his teeth. He was not used to being corrected, especially by someone as young as Macahan, and it took all his control not to lose his temper. Leaning forward, he shifted his weight in the saddle to ease the stabbing arthritic pain in his lower back and then said, 'Reckon you know why I'm here.'

'Whyn't you remind me,' Macahan said quietly. 'Just so's I got it clear in my head.'

'Very well then,' Stadtlander said. 'If that's how you want to play it, I'll oblige. You got a man in your jail. A low-life outlaw and horse-thief named Gabriel Moonlight alias Mesquite Jennings. I want him.'

' 'Mean you want to talk to him?'

'I want to hang him.'

'Ahh,' Macahan said. He swung the double-barreled scattergun off his shoulder and casually rested it across one forearm. ' 'Fraid I can't oblige you.'

'Sure you can. Look around you. There's forty of us an' only one of you.'

'I can count, Mr Stadtlander.'

'Then you can also understand that you can't stop us from takin' him.'

'I can stop *some* of you,' Macahan said pointedly. The fingers of the hand clasping the shotgun now curled around both triggers. 'Who knows . . . after your men see you an' your boy an' maybe four or five others dyin' in the dirt, they'll change their minds 'bout killin' a Deputy US Marshal just to hang a man the law will most likely hang anyway, an' turn around an' ride out of here.' As he finished talking, he swung the scattergun off his arm and leveled both barrels at Stadtlander.

Immediately the men alongside Stadtlander and Slade shifted nervously in their saddles and exchanged uneasy looks with each other.

Stadtlander never blinked. 'That case,' he said grimly, 'you better start squeezin' them triggers, 'cause we're comin' in.'

'Might want to reconsider that,' Drifter said. He and Agapita, guns held ready, stepped out of the shadows and joined Macahan on the boardwalk. The deputy didn't say anything, but he did not look happy to see them.

If he felt any fear, Stadtlander didn't show it. 'Forty against three – I still like my odds.

'This ain't poker,' Macahan warned. 'You'n your boys don't turn around, all the odds in the world won't stop a lot of you from eatin' dust.'

'Threats never won a showdown,' Stadtlander said. 'An' that's what you'll have in ten seconds.' To Slade he added, 'Start countin', son.'

Slade looked at Macahan's scattergun and nervously wet his lips. 'Pa,' he began.

'Count!' snarled his father. Then as Slade started counting down from ten, 'Last chance, Macahan.'

Macahan stood firm.

Beside him, Drifter and Agapita did the same.

Slade's tense voice droned on: '. . . five . . . four . . . three . . . two. . . . .'

Drifter saw them first. 'Wait!' he shouted. 'Hold up!'

Slade was only too happy to stop counting.

Resting his rifle on his shoulder, Drifter stepped into the street and faced the two riders coming from the livery stable.

Hearing the horses approaching, everyone but

Macahan and Stadtlander – who continued staring at each other – turned to see who it was.

The riders had now almost reached Drifter.

'Turn around,' he ordered. The color had drained from his weathered, rugged face and his voice trembled with fear and anger. 'Go back! Now!'

Emily hated to disobey her father, but she and Raven ignored him. They did not even look at each other. Eyes fixed straight ahead, expressions tight-lipped and determined, they rode past him, horses moving at a walk, and did not stop until they reached Stadtlander.

The white-haired rancher was loath to take his eyes from Macahan, but as the deputy and Agapita lowered their guns, he grudgingly turned and faced the girls.

'What do you want?' he demanded.

'My horse, El Diablo,' Emily said, loud and clear so all the townspeople peering out of windows, doorways and other hiding places could hear her. 'The horse you *stole* from me.'

'I never stole a horse from anyone in my entire *life*!' Stadtlander growled. 'Ask anyone. They'll tell you. No matter what else I've done, I ain't no horse-thief.'

'Maybe you didn't actually do the stealing yourself – you paid someone else to do that – but you certainly *knew* the stallion was stolen when you bought it, and my lawyer says that's the same thing.'

Stadtlander reddened with anger. 'I don't give two damns *what* your lawyer says. Like I told you, I bought the stallion from a reputable horse-trader and—'

'Liar.'

'Watch your mouth, girl,' Stadtlander warned. 'Or

I'll have one of my men put you over his knee.'

'Go ahead, Mr Stadtlander. Then everyone in the whole territory will know you for the bully and thief you really are.'

It was more than the hot-headed Stadtlander could take. Spurring his horse forward he spat, 'Damn you,' and went to grab Emily from her saddle – only to recoil as a shot was fired and a bullet punched a hole in his hand.

The crippled rancher yelped in pain, clutched his bloody hand to his chest and looked around to see who had fired.

Drifter, who had started forward to protect Emily, did the same.

So did everyone else.

Everyone but Latigo, that is. Six-gun already back in the holster, he smiled mockingly at the rancher.

'You!' cursed Stadtlander. Then, when Latigo didn't respond, 'What the hell's your stake in this?'

Latigo said only, 'One of you men, help him off his horse.'

Slade and the two Iverson brothers started to dismount.

Stadtlander angrily waved them back. 'Stay where you are, goddammit!'

Instantly Latigo's ivory-grip .44 Colt appeared in his left hand. He fired, once, and Slade screamed and grabbed at his right ear. The lobe was missing. His hand came away bloody. Whimpering, he started to draw – then remembering it was Latigo, stopped and began fumbling a kerchief out of his jeans.

'You goddamn bastard!' Stadtlander raged. Despite his arthritic-claw of a hand, he went for his gun.

Latigo fired, again only once, the bullet clipping the gun and knocking it from the rancher's crippled hand. He then turned to the Iverson brothers and, with a mocking smile, said, 'Mace – Cody – help your boss off his horse.'

The brothers dismounted and hurried to Stadtlander's horse.

The rancher glared defiantly at Latigo. 'You're a lousy, gutless coward,' he hissed. 'If I was twenty years younger—'

'You'd be dead,' Latigo said simply. Then to the Iversons, 'You heard me. Get him down.'

Mace and Cody carefully helped Stadtlander off the blue roan stallion.

Latigo smiled at Emily. 'Go ahead, miss. He's all yours.'

She looked at her father. Drifter, who hadn't moved, gave a nod of consent. With a squeal of joy Emily slid from her saddle, ran to El Diablo and hugged the stallion around its neck. Pressing her cheek against the blue-eyed, inky-black face, she whispered sugary terms of endearment to the horse.

Latigo said to Macahan, 'You're a witness, Deputy. Mr Stadtlander has kindly given Miss Emily back her horse.'

'At gunpoint,' Stadtlander snarled. 'Remember that, Macahan.'

'Deputy US Marshal Macahan to you, sir,' Macahan said. He turned to Drifter. 'Take the girls home, Quint.'

148

'Let's go,' Drifter told Emily and Raven.

'What about Gabe?' Raven demanded. 'We can't just run out on him.'

'He ain't goin' anywhere, missy,' Macahan told her, ' 'least, not until his trial's over.' Before she could protest, he turned to Stadtlander's men, saying, 'Go on back to the ranch, boys. We're done here for tonight.'

The riders looked at Stadtlander for permission. He glared at Macahan. 'This ain't over by a long shake. I got friends, powerful friends who make the laws in Washington. They owe me. By the time we're through with you, Deputy, you won't be able to wear a badge in a ghost town!'

'Till that time arrives,' Macahan said calmly, 'I'll try not to lose any sleep.' He watched as Slade and the Iverson brothers helped Stadtlander on to one of their horses. Cody then swung up behind his older brother and together with Slade they rode after his father and the other Double S riders.

Suddenly Main Street was empty save for the settling dust.

'Show's over, folks,' Macahan told the crowd gathered on the sidewalks. 'Go on 'bout your business.'

Grudgingly, the townspeople obeyed.

Macahan came to the edge of the boardwalk and looked at Drifter and Latigo. He spoke to Drifter first, his tone curt but not angry. 'I know you were only tryin' to help, Quint, but I warned you not to throw in with me unless you were invited. You ever butt into my duties again, I'll arrest you. Same goes for you,' he added to Latigo. 'Jerk that iron one more time in my presence,

149

an' the next sound you'll hear is a jail door slammin' behind you! We all clear on that?' Without waiting for their answer, he returned inside his office.

'... 'Be damned,' Latigo muttered, more amused than angry. 'Reckon you can't please some folks.' He paused as Emily approached. Stopping beside his horse, she gazed up at him. 'Mr Rawlins, I ... I don't know how I will ever thank you enough.'

He grinned and politely tipped his hat. 'No thanks necessary, Miss Emily. Just glad I could help.'

'Oh, you did much more than help ... you got Diablo back for me. And he is the most important thing in my life. Well,' she added, smiling at Drifter, 'the second most important thing.'

Latigo chuckled. 'You're makin' far too much out of it, Miss Emily. Ain't that right, Quint?'

'No,' Drifter said gratefully. 'I think she's got it dead right. And you can throw in my gratitude while you're at it.'

Emily said, 'See, I was right about you, Mr Rawlins. Basically, you *are* a decent man.'

'I wouldn't be spreadin' that around,' Latigo said drily. 'Might give folks the wrong impression.'

'I know I am just a schoolgirl,' she continued, 'but if there is ever anything I can do for you, Mr Rawlins, please do not hesitate to ask.'

Latigo smiled boyishly. 'There is one thing ... I'd be pleased if you'd call me by my first name. That OK with you, Quint?'

Drifter nodded.

'I hope I see you again sometime ... Latigo.'

'Hope so, too.'

'After I graduate, I am coming back here to live with my father. Maybe then we can even be friends.'

'Look forward to it,' Latigo said. He tipped his hat. 'So long, Miss Emily.' Then he wheeled his Appaloosa around and cantered off.

Emily stared after him wistfully. 'He is so-o handsome,' she said, thinking aloud. 'And so polite.'

'He's also old enough to be your father,' Drifter reminded.

'Y-yes, I suppose he is,' Emily said, as if not convinced that age mattered. 'But I will be older and more grown-up when I leave school. Besides, I find boys my own age so immature.' Turning to El Diablo, she stepped up into the saddle and kneed the blue roan alongside Raven and Agapita. 'Coming, Daddy?'

'Be right along,' Drifter said. Then to Agapita, 'Take the girls back to the stable, will you?'

'*Con mucho gusto, señor. Venga, las niñas.*'

Drifter waited until they had ridden off and then mounted the sorrel, tapped it with his spurs and rode after Latigo.

He caught up with the little Texan on the outskirts of town.

Surprised to see him, Latigo reined up. 'Forget somethin'?'

'How long we known each other, Lefty?'

'A spell. Why?'

'In all those years, I've never known you to stick your neck out for anybody.'

'So?'

'Why now? And why Emily?'

Latigo chewed on Drifter's words for a moment before saying, 'Seemed like the right thing to do.'

'Coming from you, Lefty, that's almost a joke.'

'I don't hear you laughin'.'

'That's 'cause Emily's my daughter. . . .'

'Meanin'?'

'She's got feelin's for you,' Drifter said. 'I wouldn't want it to turn into something bigger.'

Latigo gave the faintest of smiles. 'I'll try to remember that. *Adios.* . . .' He spurred his horse away.

Drifter stared after him, mind churning, and then rode back to the livery stable.

CHAPTER THIRTY

It was shortly before ten o'clock the next morning when Drifter and Emily arrived at the train station. Taking her carpetbag out of the wagon Drifter bought a one-way ticket to Las Cruces, then together they went out on to the wooden platform.

The temperature was already pushing one hundred degrees and both pulled their hats down low to shade their eyes from the broiling sun. Alongside them several other passengers were awaiting the same train. Recognizing Emily, they waved and then returned to their conversations.

For a few minutes neither Drifter nor Emily knew what to say. They looked out at the vast, sun-scorched scrubland that stretched all the way to the border and tried to think of some appropriate words – but none came.

Suddenly a roadrunner ran across the tracks and disappeared into the brush. The sight of the speedy bird seemed to break the awkward silence between them.

'I *am* doing the right thing, aren't I?' Emily said.

'Of course,' Drifter replied.

'I mean, I do not have to go back to school.'

Drifter fought back the urge to tell her to stay. 'Yes, you do. Nowadays, if you want to get ahead . . . make something special of yourself . . . you've got to have an education.'

'Yes,' Emily said dismally. 'I suppose so.'

There was another long awkward silence. Across the glinting tracks two mourning doves, startled by something in the bushes, burst aloft and winged off toward the distant heat-wavering horizon.

'I had a dove once,' Emily said. 'I rescued it from this cat in the convent garden. It had a broken wing and – and I kept it in this shoebox under my bed in my dorm. Used to feed it breadcrumbs I saved from supper.'

'What happened to it?' Drifter asked, grateful to be discussing anything but his daughter leaving.

'Sister Carmichael saw me feeding it and took it away.'

'What's so funny?' Drifter said, as Emily laughed abruptly.

'M-me. I thought she had gotten rid of it and hated her for weeks. Then one day one of the other sisters – Doherty, I think it was – told me that Sister Carmichael had kept the dove until it could fly then released it. Just shows you, doesn't it? You can be really wrong about some people.'

Drifter, trying to read her mind, said, 'If you're referring to Latigo, don't let one isolated incident turn him into Sír Galahad.'

'I'm not. Least I don't think I am.' She looked at him

154

curiously. 'You really don't like him, do you?'

'Liking or disliking him has nothing to do with it. Problem is I don't *trust* him. Too many times I've seen him turn on someone for the slightest provocation, and then kill them. Worse, he actually seems to enjoy it.'

'I know. You told me that once, when we were in Mexico.'

'Yet you still like him?' He hoped that she would quickly deny it – say that he was imagining things. Instead she frowned, puzzled, and said, 'Strange, isn't it?'

There was a distant train whistle. Shading their eyes with their hands, they looked westward along the tracks and saw black smoke billowing up into the nude blue sky.

Drifter felt a stab of anguish and caught his breath. 'Write to me, OK?'

'I already promised I would. But you have to write me back.'

'I'll do better than that. I'll come and see you.'

She nodded, a lump choking off her reply. Tears glinted in her lovely dark eyes.

'When you write, Father, be sure to tell me how Diablo is doing.'

'Definitely.'

'You could even bring him with you one day. There are stables not far from the convent. We could stall him there overnight.'

'I'll think about it.'

They could now see the train below the spiraling smoke. It seemed to be getting closer wrongfully fast.

155

'Love you, Daddy.'

'Love you too.' He felt her hug him and responded by wrapping his long arms entirely around her, squeezing her until she gave a tiny gasp. 'N-not so hard. C-can't breathe.'

He loosened his grip, saying, 'Just trying to make up for all those hugs you told me you'd missed.'

Emily laughed through her tears and, reaching up on tiptoe, pressed her wet cheek against his. He smelled her hair, warm and fresher than new-cut hay; felt her skin, smoother than any marble statue he'd ever seen.

At that moment, though he didn't know how to tell her, he loved her more than life itself.

Later, as the train was pulling out, Emily waved goodbye to him from one of the windows.

Drifter waved back. Inside, it felt as if barbed wire was tugging at his heart.

He stood there, sun hot on his shoulders, watching the train speed away, long after Emily had stopped leaning out of the window. Then, heavy-hearted, he walked to the end of the platform, stepped on to the warm yellow dirt and headed for the wagon.

When he reached it, he heard a horse approaching from the other side of the little station house. He turned and to his surprise, saw it was Latigo.

'You been here all this time?'

Latigo nodded. 'Wanted to make sure Emily got off safely.'

'She would have loved to have said goodbye to you.'

'I ain't big on goodbyes.' There was a gruffness in his voice that suggested he was covering up his emotions.

It came to Drifter then and immediately after the thought hit him, he cursed himself for not realizing it before.

'It was for her – Emily,' he said, 'wasn't it?'

Latigo frowned, as if not understanding.

'Why you stopped me from breaking Gabe out of jail. You wanted to make sure her old man didn't end up behind bars.'

'I got no idea what you're talkin' about,' Latigo said, rolling a smoke.

'Sure you don't.' Drifter smiled without humor. 'Word ever got around that you actually cared for somebody, it would destroy your image. Might even get you killed.'

Latigo stuck the cigarette between his parched lips, flared a match, cocked his head to avoid the flame, puffed and flipped away the match. Then he pulled a folded envelope out of his shirt pocket and handed it to Drifter.

'Give this to Gabe next time you see him.'

'What is it?'

'He'll know when he reads it.' Latigo wheeled his horse about. 'See ya around, *amigo*,' and rode off, on across the railroad tracks, toward Mexico.

'*Via con Dios*,' Drifter called after him.

Twenty minutes later he stood beside Gabriel Moonlight's locked cell, watching his friend reading the contents of the envelope.

'Dammit,' he said finally. 'You gonna tell me what it says?'

Gabe looked up, gave a huge grin and passed the document through the bars. 'See for yourself.'

Drifter eagerly read the page. Typed on a Sholes & Glidden Type Writer on expensive ivory-colored paper bearing the letterhead of Sharpe, Wintergreen and McPherson, 473 E. Pine St., Deming, New Mexico, the document spelled out the involvement of Latigo Rawlins and Stillman J. Stadtlander in the murders of five Mexican ranchers. A lot of legalese made it difficult to fully understand and Drifter, who needed reading glasses, had to squint to read it. But once he had grasped the meaning of the contents, he knew instantly that Latigo – whose signature was scrawled at the bottom – had not only incriminated himself but in the process had given Gabriel the ammunition to force Stadtlander to drop all charges against him – or face the consequences.

'Judas,' Drifter said, looking up. 'This is some hot potato.'

'What d'you make of it?' Gabriel asked.

'You mean why did Lefty do it?'

Gabriel nodded. 'It ain't like him, Quint. Ain't like him at all.'

'Lately,' Drifter said, thinking of Emily, 'Mr Rawlins has been doing a *lot* of things that ain't like him.'

'You don't sound too happy about it.'

'Oh, I'm happy about it – for you anyway.'

'Then quit lookin' so goddamn glum. I mean, what the hell, Quint, soon I'll be a free man again an' then me'n Ingrid can get married.'

Drifter grimaced. Marriage was the last word he needed to hear.